PEN PALS
BOOK TWO

PALMER AT YOUR SERVICE

by Sharon Dennis Wyeth

A YEARLING BOOK

Published by
Dell Publishing
a division of
Bantam Doubleday Dell Publishing Group, Inc.
666 Fifth Avenue
New York, New York 10103

The trademark Yearling ® is registered in the U.S. Patent and Trademark Office.
ISBN: 0-440-40343-X

Published by arrangement with Parachute Press, Inc.
Printed in the United States of America
June 1990
10 9 8 7 6 5 4 3 2 1
OPM

For my parents, Evon Dennis Bush and Creed Dennis, Jr., and in memory of my singing teacher, Graham Bernard

CHAPTER ONE

"I am so brilliant!" said Palmer Durand with a flip of her wavy blond hair. "Look at this! I just solved all my parent problems."

Palmer handed two letters to her roommate, Amy Ho. Both the letters were written on flowered blue paper in Palmer's distinctive curlicued handwriting.

Amy kicked off her short black boots and plopped down on her neatly made bed. The two girls shared a room in a suite at the Alma Stephens Boarding School for Girls.

"What are you up to, Palmer?" Amy asked, noticing the twinkle in her roommate's blue eyes.

Palmer grinned mischievously. "Read!" she said, pointing to the letters.

Dear Mom,

Maybe you have gotten the announcement from Miss Pryn's office about the Parents' Weekend here at Alma Stephens coming up soon. I'm pretty sure Daddy is coming, so I won't blame you if you decide not to.

I was wondering about my allowance. Do you think you could raise it by thirty dollars? Thanks in advance.

Love,
Palmer

P.S. How's the weather down there in Florida? Up here in New Hampshire it's freezing!

"Nice letter," said Amy, shifting onto her elbow. "But do you really think she'll up your allowance? You're already the richest girl in Fox Hall."

"You can never have enough money," Palmer said carelessly. "Read the other letter."

Amy picked up the second piece of blue stationery.

Dear Daddy,
Maybe you have gotten the announcement from Miss Pryn's office about the Parents' Weekend here at Alma coming up soon. I thought you might like to know that I think Mom is coming, so I'm sure you won't want to come also.

I was wondering about my allowance. I could use about thirty more dollars a month. Thanks in advance.

Love,
Palmer

P.S. How's the weather in California? It was warm here, but now it's turned cold.

Amy handed the letter back with a puzzled smile. "I don't get it," she said, running her fingers through her spiky black hair. "Why did you write both your parents the same thing? I can understand your asking each of them for a raise in your allowance, but if they each think the other one is coming for Parents' Weekend, *neither* of them will show up."

"That's the idea," Palmer said.

Amy reached beneath her bed and pulled out an instrument case. "I couldn't keep my parents away," she said, taking out her brand-new dulcimer and starting to tune it. "Ever since I came to Alma, my dad's been chomping at the bit to check things out here. At home, he always kept an eagle eye on me."

"My dad likes keeping his eye on me, too," said Palmer, "but this time I'm not going to give him the chance."

"I think you're making a mistake," said Amy. "Parents' Weekend will probably be fun."

"Maybe for you," said Palmer, crossing to her closet. "You don't have parent problems."

"Did I hear someone say something about parent problems?" a voice rang out from the sitting room.

"We're in here discussing them right now, Lisa," yelled Amy.

The third resident of Suite 3-D walked into Amy and Palmer's room. Lisa McGreevy's pretty face was flushed from the cold and her dark eyes were sparkling.

"I don't get this weather," Lisa muttered, blowing on her half-frozen fingers. "One day it's like the Bahamas, and the next it's like the North Pole."

"Palmer's not inviting her mom and dad to Parents' Weekend," Amy announced.

Lisa tossed her parka on Amy's bed. "How come, Palmer?"

"You probably wouldn't understand," said Palmer, "just like Amy doesn't. You both have perfect parents who think everything you do is wonderful."

"Hold on," said Amy. "I never said *that* about my parents."

3

"I wouldn't say it about mine either," said Lisa, sitting down to take off her boots. "But speaking of wonderful, wait till you hear about my new assignment for art!" she went on, changing the subject. "It's really challenging."

"What is it?" Amy asked.

"I have to paint a portrait," said Lisa.

"A portrait of who?" Palmer asked, looking interested.

"Anyone I want," Lisa replied.

Palmer flashed a brilliant smile. "How about me? I've always wanted to have my picture painted."

"Well," Lisa said doubtfully. She knew how hard to please Palmer could be, and she didn't want to make her project any more difficult than it had to be. "Actually, I was thinking about Amy," she hedged. "She has such an interesting face."

"Count me out," Amy said, plucking her dulcimer. "I'm not the model type."

"Then maybe I'd better paint Shanon," Lisa said hastily. "Since we share a room, that will making working together easier."

"But Shanon's so busy," Palmer protested. "She's hardly ever here anymore. Don't forget, she's got that new job at the student-run ice-cream parlor, The Tuck Store."

"You mean The Tuck Shop," Amy corrected her.

"Whatever," said Palmer. "And not only that, Shanon spends tons of time writing for *The Ledger*, whereas I have all the time in the world! Besides, I—"

"Okay, okay!" Lisa chuckled. "I can see you really want to get your picture painted, so you can be the model."

"Great," said Palmer, jumping to her feet. "I'd better check out my closet for something fabulous to wear."

"Relax," said Lisa. "I can't start until tomorrow. I have loads of studying to do after dinner."

"Me, too," said Amy.

"Not me," Palmer said, making a face, "Brenda Smith and I are watching a movie."

"Are you sure you shouldn't be studying, too?" Amy said with concern. "Remember Miss Grayson's comments on your last French paper."

Palmer's face turned pink. "All right," she said. "I'll study my French . . . *after* I watch the movie. I—" Palmer broke off in mid-sentence at the sound of the outside door slamming shut.

"Hi, everybody!" a cheerful voice called.

"Hi, Shanon!" Lisa yelled. "We're in here! In Palmer and Amy's room!"

Shanon Davis crossed through the sitting room of Suite 3-D and poked her head in. The fourth of the suitemates, Shanon was also the youngest. She had grown up in the nearby town of Brighton and had come to Alma on scholarship.

"What a day!" she said. Pulling off her orange knit cap, she ran a hand through her sandy brown hair. "Working at The Tuck Shop is incredible!"

"Are you exhausted?" asked Lisa.

"No, just stuffed," Shanon giggled. "Full of free ice cream."

"You get free ice cream?" exclaimed Amy. "Nice job."

"I'll say," said Palmer, turning away from the mirror. "Still, I wouldn't want to be a waitress. It must be horrible."

"It's not horrible at all," Shanon declared. "It's fun. Everything at The Tuck Shop is basically run by students. Of

5

course, Mrs. Butter does come around to supervise," she said. Like most of the Alma girls, Shanon often referred to the school cook and dietician, Mrs. Worth, by her nickname. "I almost forgot," she added, pulling some envelopes out of her jacket. "I stopped by Booth Hall and—"

"Mail!" cried Lisa, jumping up. "Did I get a letter from Rob? I did!" she squealed, spying one of the envelopes. "I recognize his handwriting!"

"I should hope so," Shanon teased, handing her the letter. "Rob Williams has only been your pen pal since the start of the school year."

"I see I got a letter from John," Amy exclaimed, crowding in. "I love the way he makes his *A*'s," she added, grabbing the envelope.

Shanon giggled again. "You mean *A* as in Amy?"

Amy blushed. "Yes, I guess so."

"What about my pen pal?" Palmer asked, crossing to Shanon. "Did I get a letter from Sam?"

"Sorry," said Shanon. "I didn't get one from Mars either."

"Oh, well," Palmer said with a shrug, "I only wrote Sam yesterday."

"You'll probably hear from him soon," Shanon assured her.

"Listen to this!" cried Lisa, waving Rob's letter in front of her friends' faces.

Dear Lisa,

In this snowy desert you are like a rare flower. The greatest moment of my life comes when I open a big fat letter

*from you. Do you know how many times I read the things
you write me? Millions—*

"Good grief," snickered Palmer. "Is that ever corny!"
"Let me finish," Lisa said with smile.

*Hah—gotcha, McGreevy! Did you think I was going to
write you a gooey letter? I bet you did. I'm just trying out
a new style. By the way, that perfume you put on your last
letter is very nice. The only problem is, it made my blazer
smell like a perfume store. Mars started ribbing me about it,
but I lied and told him I was wearing a men's after-shave.
Thanks for writing that I look like a movie star.*

Yours,
Rob

"Did you really tell him he looked like a movie star?"
asked Palmer.
"Why not?" Lisa sighed. "It's true. Rob is so tall and
good-looking, and I guess if he wears after-shave, that must
mean that he's shaving, and—"
"Do you mind if I read my letter from John now?" Amy
interrupted.
"Of course, Amy," Lisa said guiltily. "It's your turn."

Dear Amy,
  Happy Chinese New Year.
  Here is a poem for you.
      Digging up the last season flowers
      Reaching into my mind for something
      Amazing

Grantastic
On this unordinary day, I found a worm and
Named it Mars.

Yours,
John

P.S. *The poem is in your honor.*

"That is hysterical!" said Lisa. "A worm and he named it after his roommate."

"I wonder if Mars saw it," Shanon giggled. "Those two guys are always kidding each other."

"But what does it have to do with you, Amy?" Palmer asked, reading the poem again.

Amy smiled. "It's another one of John's acrostics. See," she said, pointing to the first letter of each line. "The acrostic is *dragon*. He did that because according to the Chinese zodiac, I was born in the year of the dragon."

"Neat," said Lisa. "It's so much fun to get letters from our pen pals. I just wish we could see them more often!"

"Me, too," said Palmer. "But at least your pen pals go to Ardsley Academy. You get to see them whenever the two schools sponsor joint activities. I wish Sam had never transferred to the Brighton public school. It's even harder for us to get together."

"There's a chance we could see them all soon," Shanon said eagerly. "*The Ledger* is holding a fund-raising mixer next month, and boys are definitely invited—no matter where they go to school. All they have to do is buy tickets."

"I heard about that," said Amy. "There's only one problem. It's on the same night as the Parents' Weekend dinner for third-formers."

"Why should that be a problem?" objected Lisa. "We can

have dinner with our parents and then take them over to the dance and introduce them to our pen pals."

"Great!" said Shanon. "I really want Mars to meet my father. I think they'll like each other a lot."

"I want my parents to meet John, too," Amy agreed.

"And I'm sure Rob and my folks will hit it off," added Lisa. "I'm going to write and invite him tomorrow."

"And I'll invite Sam O'Leary," Palmer chimed in. "Of course, we'll get to spend the whole evening together at the dance, since my parents won't be here for Parents' Weekend."

"Your parents aren't coming?" said Shanon. "That's too bad."

"She didn't invite them," volunteered Amy.

"Why not?" Shanon said, looking bewildered.

Palmer lowered her big blue eyes. "Let's just say I have my reasons."

CHAPTER TWO

Lisa sat up straight in her chair and stared out of the big library window. Beyond it, the courtyard was soggy with half-melted snow. Lisa yawned and put aside her Latin vocabulary list. She'd been studying for a whole hour. It was time for a break. Carefully taking a piece of paper from her notebook, she started to write:

Dear Rob,

Roses are red, violets are blue . . . Tricked you! Yes, the beginning of your letter was quite gooey, and please don't make fun of my perfume. Anyway, I didn't put perfume on the paper, I used scented stationery.

Lots of neat things are going on here at Alma. I guess it's because this month our school will be one hundred years old and a lot of activities have been planned around the Centennial. First of all, there's a fund-raising mixer for our school paper, The Ledger, *which will also be one hundred years old this month. Would you like to come to that? It costs money, but it is for a good cause. Shanon, Amy, Palmer, and I are definitely going to be there. Since that is the same night as the Parents' Weekend dinner for third-formers, I will have my parents with me, however! I hope you don't mind, but I'd really like to introduce you to them. Please write and let me know if you want to come.*

Love,
Lisa

Shanon tapped her foot impatiently beneath the desk in *The Ledger* office. She was trying to write an article for the special Centennial issue. But at the moment she had nothing to say. Kate Majors, the assistant editor, had asked for something humorous. But unlike her "wild and crazy" pen pal, Mars Martinez, Shanon had always found it hard to be funny. Just thinking of Mars made Shanon smile, however. She always had plenty to say to him. . . .

Dear Mars,

Help! I am supposed to write a funny story for the 100th anniversary issue of The Ledger, *and I can't think of anything. Any ideas? I also wanted to invite you to* The Ledger *fund-raising mixer. My mom and dad will be visiting Alma that weekend, so if you come to the dance you will also get to meet them. I think you'll like my dad. He's funny just like you are. I can hardly wait to see my parents. I miss them, even though they live just a few miles away from Alma.*

Write soon,
Shanon

P.S. Palmer did not invite her mom and dad to her Parents' Weekend. I think she's kind of weird.

Shanon quickly scanned the letter. She was pleased with what she'd written until she got to the last part where she called Palmer weird. It wasn't nice, Shanon decided, to write something like that about her suitemate, even in a private letter to Mars. And taking another piece of paper from her folder, she copied the letter over, leaving out the P.S.

In a booth at the language lab, Amy took off one pair of earphones and reached for another. She'd heard enough Spanish vocabulary words and sentences. Now it was time for a break. She put on the earphones attached to her own Walkman, and the music of New Kids on the Block filled her ears. As she tapped her fingers on the smooth desk inside the cubicle, Amy thought that New Kids was just the kind of group John Adams would like. It had been a long time since Amy and her tall, cute, redheaded pen pal had talked music. Reaching into her bookbag, she got out a paper and pen.

Dear John,

You have a radical mind. Only you would think of such a unique way to wish me a happy new year. I loved the acrostic.

I am finding my new dulcimer very inspiring, although I do still play my guitar a lot. I have written a new song! I don't know when I can play it for you, though. How would you like to come to a dance? The Ledger is selling tickets to one. It's on the same weekend that my parents will be up here. I might be able to play my new song for you then, although I will probably be too busy with my parents to go back to the lounge. Besides, my dad is pretty unreasonable about me and my music. He doesn't want to hear that I like rock and roll and he really doesn't want to hear that I'm a songwriter. As far as he is concerned, I will either be a scientist or go into business when I grow up.

12

I hear Ardsley's hockey team is very good. Alma's isn't bad either. What music are you into these days? Right now I like New Kids on the Block. Let me know if you're coming to the mixer.

Yours truly,
Amy

P.S. It was pretty funny when you called Mars a worm in your poem. Good thing he's got a sense of humor. My roommate Palmer would not think this was funny!

Palmer chewed idly on her fingernails. The Misty Mauve polish she'd applied just the day before was almost all worn off. She picked up her notebook and began fanning her flushed face. Even though it was chilly in the hallway, she was starting to perspire. She'd been waiting outside Mr. Griffith's office for nearly twenty minutes. Dan Griffith was not only her English teacher, but her third-form advisor as well. Three days ago, he'd asked Palmer to make an appointment.

Palmer looked up anxiously as Mr. Griffith stuck his head out of the door of his office. "Sorry, Palmer," he said. "I'm running a little late with my last conference. Can you wait a few more minutes?"

"Sure," Palmer answered, trying not to look worried.

As soon as Mr. Griffith went back into his office, Palmer leafed through her assignment book. Her math homework had been due the day before and she hadn't even started it. Her essay for English was due at the end of the week and she still didn't have a topic. And then there was a new list of French vocabulary to memorize. Turning to a blank page, she started to doodle. Before she knew it, she was writing to Sam.

13

Dear Sam,

I hate studying. Don't you? There are so many more interesting things we could do with our time. Maybe I should be like you and transfer to Brighton. A public school is probably a lot easier than a place like Alma or Ardsley. And we can't all be brains like Shanon Davis!!

How are things going with your band? I love The Fantasy's music more than anything! By the way, there is going to be a fund-raising mixer here. I was wondering if you—

The door to Mr. Griffith's office opened once more, and Muffin Talbot walked out.

"All right, Palmer," Mr. Griffith said. "You're next."

Palmer smiled nervously and glanced at the young English teacher's green eyes. They looked very serious. And Mr. Griffith definitely wasn't smiling.

CHAPTER THREE

"Stop wiggling," said Lisa, glaring over the easel she'd set up in the sitting room.

"Sorry," said Palmer. "I can't stop thinking about what Mr. Griffith said in my conference."

Lisa put down her paintbrush. "I guess I'd be worried, too," she admitted. "Getting an academic warning sounds serious."

"It *is* serious," Palmer moaned. "It means that if one more teacher says I'm not doing well, I'll be put on probation—or even worse! I've got to figure some way out of this."

"That's easy," said Lisa, starting to paint again. "Just study harder. It's not as if Mr. Griffith or Miss Grayson or any of the other teachers want to give you bad reports. The teachers are here to help us."

Palmer rolled her eyes. "Then why do they teach boring subjects like French and English and all that other stuff? Why can't they teach something exciting? Something that doesn't have so much homework?"

"Like what?" said Lisa.

"How should I know?" Palmer said dispiritedly. "Like . . . sword fighting!"

Lisa chuckled. "I'm sure there would be homework in sword fighting, too. Fencing takes a lot of practice. The trouble with you, Palmer, is that the minute you think something's hard you give up on it."

Palmer shrugged her shoulders and stretched. "You're right. I do. But what's the point? I'm not a brain, and everyone knows it."

"Cheer up," said Lisa. "Come and see your portrait."

Palmer walked over and peered at Lisa's canvas. "That doesn't look like me."

"I've barely started," said Lisa.

"Those aren't my eyebrows," Palmer said critically. "I have very thin eyebrows, not thick ones."

"Will you please leave the eyebrows to me," Lisa grumbled. "This is *my* art project."

"Hey, guys," said Amy, letting herself into the suite. She threw down her black leather jacket and took a look at Lisa's picture. "Wow!" she exclaimed. "Great painting. It looks a little like Madonna."

"Thanks," said Lisa. "I'm glad somebody likes it."

Amy shook out her muffler. "It's drizzling. Every day something new and strange falls from the sky. It's already dark, and it's only four o'clock."

Palmer looked out the window. "Yuk," she muttered.

"It's not that bad," Amy said, picking up her guitar. "Tonight we're having pepper steak for dinner."

"Yum!" said Lisa. "I love Mrs. Butter's pepper steak."

"You can have mine," Palmer said dramatically. "I couldn't eat a thing tonight. Not even hamburger and ice cream." She plopped down on the loveseat and buried her head under a cushion.

"What's wrong with Palmer?" Amy whispered.

16

"She's been given an academic warning," Lisa said softly.

"I heard you," said Palmer. "You don't have to whisper about it. Soon the whole world will know."

Amy sat down on the other end of the loveseat. "What awful news," she said sympathetically. "What are you going to do about it?"

Palmer smiled weakly. "Start studying for a change. Will you help me?"

"Of course I will," Amy said.

"And I'll help, too," Lisa offered. "Of course, the only subjects I'm good at are art and history. Shanon could help you with Latin and French, though."

"I'll quiz you on your math homework," Amy promised.

Palmer cheered up immediately. "Thanks, you guys," she said, tossing the cushion onto the floor. "With you helping me, I'm sure to improve. To tell the truth, I had a feeling something like this might be happening. I've been really letting things slide."

"I kind of noticed that," said Amy. "I haven't seen you open a book in weeks."

"But even when I do study, all I can come up with is a C minus," Palmer said glumly. "So then I wonder what's the point of studying at all."

"There's a lot of point to it," Lisa exclaimed. "Getting a C minus is a lot better than failing altogether."

"I know," Palmer mumbled. "I just wish my parents felt that way."

Amy looked puzzled. "What are you talking about?"

"It's my stepsister, Georgette," Palmer said, sitting up to explain. "She's my father's second wife's daughter."

"What about her?" asked Lisa.

"Well," said Palmer. "Georgette is a total brain. She's A + all the way. How do you think that makes me look to my father?"

"I can see how that would be rough," said Amy.

"There's no way that I'm ever going to be an A student," Palmer went on. "That's the reason I didn't want my parents to come to the big weekend."

"You haven't told them about your meeting with Mr. Griffith?" Lisa asked.

Palmer shook her head. "They think I'm doing okay in my grades."

"Gosh," said Amy, "when they find out you're on academic warning—"

"They won't," Palmer broke in. "I'm going to work really hard to bring my grades up. There's no way Mom and Dad are going to take me out of here."

Lisa's eyes widened. "Take you *out* of here?"

"They wouldn't do that!" exclaimed Amy.

"They might," Palmer said sadly. "They transferred me in grammar school two times, and I lost all my friends. It was awful."

"Well, we're not going to let that happen this time," Amy said firmly. "Right, Lisa?"

"Of course not," Lisa said. Then, glancing at Palmer, she added, "Most of it's going to be up to you, though."

"Don't worry," Palmer said confidently. "From now on, I'm going to do nothing but study, study, study. I'll bring my grades up to all A's before my parents ever even know I've been on warning." She stood up from the loveseat just as Shanon walked into the suite.

"Guess what?" Shanon said with a grin. "Mars sent me a message over the computer in *The Ledger* office."

"Oh, my gosh!" squeaked Lisa. "I hope Kate doesn't find out."

"That's right," Amy said. "Remember the trouble we got into the last time we used the computer for socializing."

"Don't worry," said Shanon. "This was strictly newspaper business. I asked Mars for some help with a story for the Centennial issue and he was just giving me some advice."

"Oh, that's different," Lisa said. "Even Kate couldn't object to that."

"I came to get you for dinner," said Shanon, dropping her books on the desk. "Are you ready to go?"

"You bet!" said Amy. "Bring on that pepper steak."

"Just a minute," said Palmer. Crossing to her bedroom, she pulled off her turtleneck. "I want to change."

"Hurry it up," Lisa said, grabbing her parka.

"By the way," Shanon said, following Palmer into her room. "There were three letters for you in your mailbox."

"Three?" Palmer gasped in delight. "I bet one is from Sam, right?"

"I think I recognize his handwriting," Shanon said with a smile as she handed Palmer the envelopes.

"Who are the other two from?" Amy asked from the doorway.

"My mother and father," Palmer replied, checking the return addresses.

"Read them at dinner," Lisa begged. "My stomach is growling."

"All right," Palmer agreed. "I'll bring them with me. Better still," she said, rummaging through her closet, "why don't you all go ahead. I'll meet you there."

"We'll save you a seat," Lisa said, out the front door like a shot.

"See you later," Amy and Shanon chorused.

"See you," Palmer called. "And thanks for bringing the mail."

As soon as her suitemates were gone, Palmer headed straight for Sam's letter. She still planned to take the mail with her to the dining hall, but she couldn't wait till then to open it. Picturing Sam O'Leary's reddish blond hair and romantic gray eyes, she tore open the envelope.

Dear Palmer,

In your last letter you mentioned the fund-raising mixer for The Ledger. *Thanks for inviting me, but you didn't have to. I will definitely be there, because Sam and The Fantasy has been hired as the band that night. It will be great to see you again!*

Also in your letter you said that you thought Brighton must be easier than Alma. I don't know if that's true. Brighton has very high standards. I have to work at least as hard here as I did when I went to Ardsley Academy. It's not just a good public school, it's a good school. I know what you mean about studying being boring, but I guess I'm used to it because I don't really mind it.

See you at the mixer!

Sam

Sam's letter was great news! As she smiled at her reflection in the mirror over her bureau, Palmer imagined how cool Sam would look sitting behind his drums. Maybe he would come up to the microphone and dedicate a song to her! Then he would come down from the stage and ask her to dance.

Humming a little song, she dashed over to her closet and pulled out a pale peach silk blouse. Then she slipped out of her wool slacks and into a skirt. She was feeling so great that it was hard to remember how unhappy she'd been after her conference with Mr. Griffith. She had made a decision to study hard and her suitemates were going to help her bring up her grades . . . and best of all, she was going to see her pen pal again. Sam would be the star of the mixer, and Palmer would be the envy of everyone!

As she hurriedly ran a brush through her hair, she noticed the two envelopes from her parents lying on the dresser. Probably more good news, Palmer thought cheerfully. She had asked both her mother and father for a raise in her allowance. With any luck at all, they had probably both sent her some money!

Pausing by the door, she opened the envelopes:

Dear Palmer,

I have talked to your mother and I will be coming to Parents' Weekend. As for your allowance, we'll discuss your finances then.

Love,
Dad

Dear Palmer,

I just spoke to your father, and I will definitely be coming to Parents' Weekend. The two of us are meeting in Boston and traveling on to New Hampshire together. We think it is important.

Love,
Mom

P.S. About the raise in allowance, I'll have to give it some thought.

CHAPTER FOUR

—◆—

Dear Mars,

Thanks for contacting me over the computer. I think your idea about digging into the social life of Alma girls a hundred years ago and comparing it to what we do today is a terrific one. Imagine what they would have thought of a disco weenie roast back in the old days? I am glad you are coming to the mixer. Hope you'll like my dad.

Yours truly,
Shanon

Dear Lisa,

The mixer sounds cool. I am sort of nervous about meeting your mom and dad, though. Of course, if they're anything like you, I'm sure they'll be nice.

See you then,
Rob

Dear Amy,

Too bad your parents don't know how talented you are as a budding rock artist. But I have an idea. I hear that Sam

and The Fantasy are playing at the mixer (which I am com-
ing to—thanks for the invite!). Since Sam's an old pal of
mine from when he went to Ardsley, I could ask him to play
one of your songs, maybe "Cabin Fever." Then your dad
would hear what a great talent you are. What do you think?

Sincerely,
John

P.S. In the meantime, how about sending me a tape of your
new song?

"Perfect," said Lisa. "Now all our pen pals are coming!"

"I can't wait," said Amy. "My mom and dad are really interested in meeting John."

"I'm sure they'll like him," said Lisa. "John is the perfect Ardie."

"He certainly looks like the perfect Ardie," Amy said, her dark eyes twinkling. "For that matter, so does Rob."

"Well, Mars doesn't look like the perfect Ardie," said Shanon, remembering the time her pen pal showed up at an Alma dance wearing a white T-shirt and string tie beneath his blue blazer. "It's a good thing my dad is the informal type," she added. "He'll like Mars no matter what he ends up wearing."

"I'm glad you three have everything all worked out," Palmer said, nervously pacing the sitting-room floor. "Before my parents get here, we've really got to clean out this bookshelf," she scolded. "If there's anything my mother hates, it's disorganization."

Lisa eyed the bookshelf in the corner. Besides the four girls' schoolbooks, notebooks, and papers, it was cluttered with stacks of magazines and photographs.

"I think most of the magazines are yours," Lisa pointed

out to Palmer. "And at least four of the pictures on top are of Sam and The Fantasy. If anyone cleans out the bookshelf, it should be you."

"How can I?" wailed Palmer. "I haven't got time. Besides sitting for the portrait you're painting that doesn't look a thing like me, I've got homework up to my ears. I can't believe my parents are actually coming next week! I'll have to work night and day if I'm going to raise my grades before they get here." And with that, Palmer threw herself on the loveseat and shut her eyes.

There was a moment of silence as the other three girls looked at her sympathetically.

"I don't think you can change your grades in just one week," Shanon finally ventured.

"I have to," Palmer moaned.

"Face it, Palmer," said Lisa. "That's impossible."

"Why don't you just let your parents know that even though you've messed up in most of your subjects, you've decided to improve," Amy suggested. "All they can do is ask you to try harder."

"That isn't all they can do," Palmer said. "Remember, they could transfer me out of here."

Again the suite was filled with silence.

"That would be awful," Shanon said quietly. "It just wouldn't be the same without you, Palmer."

"No, it wouldn't," Lisa agreed. "The Foxes of the Third Dimension has four people in it, not three," she said, referring to her suitemates by the code name they used when they first advertised for boy pen pals in the Ardsley newspaper.

"I think you're worried about nothing," Amy said bluntly. "Your own mother went to school at Alma Stephens, Palmer. She's not going to pull you out."

"She might," Palmer said stubbornly. "I know she doesn't think Alma is strict enough."

"Not strict enough!?" Lisa exclaimed.

"We can't even go to class without wearing a skirt," Amy protested. "And forget any kind of social life. If it wasn't for our pen pals, we wouldn't have one at all."

"Still," said Palmer, "things are a lot more liberal now than they were in Mother's day. And I'm just afraid that . . ." Her voice trailed off with a sigh.

"Listen, Palmer," Lisa said encouragingly. "There are other areas that people can do well in besides academics. You're pretty good at sports. Won't your parents like that?"

"Mom *was* sort of a jock when she went here," Palmer said. "I have done well in gym, at least—and tennis," she added, perking up again.

"Not to mention that you've got three great suitemates," Amy added. "That should count for something with your parents. My mom and dad were very concerned about the kind of girls I'd meet here. They wanted to make sure I was going to school with nice people."

"That stuff matters to my parents, too," Palmer said eagerly. "And they couldn't possibly say anything bad about you guys . . . especially if Amy changes her hairstyle!"

"What?" said Amy. "I'm not changing my hair for anyone!"

"You have to," said Palmer. "When my mother and father see you with your hair sticking up in that strange way, they'll definitely take me out of here."

"No, they won't," said Amy. "That's ridiculous."

"I think so, too," Lisa said. "Your parents will know that Amy's not weird as soon as they talked to her. Besides, they'll be too busy paying attention to you to notice how the rest of us wear our hair."

Palmer sighed. "I guess you're right. They're going to be on me like glue, asking me all about everything. They'll definitely find out I've been goofing off. I just thought that if everything in the suite looked perfect and if you guys looked perfect and spent a lot of time talking to them—"

"Hold on," said Shanon, who'd been mostly listening until then. "We'll do our best to make a good impression but it's going to be up to you to explain your grades."

Lisa nodded. "There's no way you're going to get out of it."

"One good thing," Amy reminded her, "is that Sam will be there."

"That's right!" exclaimed Palmer. "When they see Sam onstage at the mixer, my parents will be really impressed."

"Everybody's impressed with Sam," Shanon agreed. "He's really nice—and also talented!"

"Not only that," Lisa added, "Sam's an Ardie! Didn't your father go to Ardsley when he was young, Palmer?"

"Well . . . yes," Palmer answered doubtfully, "but Sam isn't exactly an Ardie anymore. He transferred to the public school in Brighton last semester."

"What difference does that make?" Lisa said. "Once an Ardie, always an Ardie. My dad went to Ardsley, too. That school loyalty stuff is really important to him."

Shanon giggled. "My dad couldn't care less about what schools people go to. All he cares about is what their favorite team is . . . that and whether they know how to change a tire. I bet those are the first two things he asks Mars."

"*Can* Mars change a tire?" Lisa asked with a laugh.

"I don't know," said Shanon. "But I'll probably find out the night of the dinner. I just hope Dad doesn't challenge him to a tire-changing contest."

Palmer got up and headed toward her bedroom.

"Ready to go over your math homework?" Amy asked.

"In a little while," Palmer said. "I've got some thinking to do first."

Alone in the room she shared with Amy, Palmer closed the door softly behind her and sank down on her bed. No matter how much she tried to look on the bright side of things, she couldn't stop worrying about her parents' visit. It had been such a long time since Palmer had seen her mother and father, and she was almost never with them together. What a bummer that they were coming all this way just to find out what a failure she was!

There was only one thing to do, Palmer thought. Amy was right. Before she saw her parents, she had to tell them the truth. If they knew she was sorry and was going to try harder, maybe they wouldn't be angry. Maybe they wouldn't be too disappointed.

She got off the bed and marched briskly to her desk. Then, she carefully composed a letter.

Dear Mom and Dad,

I got your letters. I guess I should tell you before you get here that I am not doing too well in a lot of my subjects. I am very, very sorry. But I have turned over a new leaf and am trying very hard now. Wait until you meet Amy, Lisa, and Shanon. They are the perfect Alma girls! Mom, you will like them. They are very smart. Also, when you come you will get to meet my pen pal! His name is Sam O'Leary and he is very smart also. He will be providing the entertainment. Dad, you will like him because he is an Ardie!

Love,
Palmer

P.S. I really need a raise in my allowance.

Palmer quickly stuffed the letter into an envelope, but paused before addressing it. She wondered where to send the letter—to her mother or to her father. If only she could write one address on the envelope for both her parents. If only they lived in the same place!

But Palmer knew that was impossible. Taking a second piece of blue stationery, she copied the letter over and then addressed two separate envelopes. One would go to California and the other to Florida.

Meanwhile, Amy was addressing an envelope of her own. But it would only be going a few miles down the road—to Ardsley Academy.

Dear John,

Thanks for your idea about asking Sam to sing one of our songs, but no thanks. Like I said, my dad doesn't want to hear anything about my liking rock music. Here's the cassette of my new song you asked for and a copy of the lyrics:

Stage Boy Blues
Up the stairs, like a comet I spring
I'm the one who fixes the stage
Through the squeak of the mikes,
I can hear my whole life
I've got the stage boy blues.
Oh, at night I sweep up the floor
Where the fans have their popcorn poured
Oh, I collect tickets and wish it had been me
I'm just the one who cleans up, the utility truck
If only you could hear me sing
I've got the stage boy blues.

CHAPTER FIVE

The dining hall was festively decorated with large vases of pink and white flowers the night of the third-formers' dinner on Parents' Weekend. Amy's, Shanon's, and Lisa's parents had already arrived, but Palmer's parents had called from the Boston airport to say they'd be late.

"Where are they?" Palmer muttered anxiously as she and Amy stood in the foyer near the front door.

"Don't worry," said Amy. "They'll be here." She gave Palmer's elbow a gentle squeeze. "The way you tried to stop your mom and dad from showing up at all, I'd think you'd be glad for the delay."

"I'm still worried about what they'll say about my grades," Palmer admitted, fiddling with the bow on her pink dress. "But now that I know they're coming, I can't wait to see them. I don't want them to miss the dinner."

She glanced into the dining room at the circular table where Lisa and Shanon were already seated with their parents. Amy's mother and father were there, too. "You can go sit with your folks," Palmer said to Amy. "You don't have to wait out here with me."

"I want to wait with you," Amy said loyally. "Mom and Dad won't mind. They seem to be getting along fine with Shanon's parents."

Palmer peeked back into the dining room. Mr. Davis had just told a joke, and all the other parents were laughing. "Shanon's father is great," she said. "Maybe he'll tell so many jokes tonight that my parents will forget all about my grades."

"Or at least get into a good mood," added Amy. "Then, even if they do bring up your grades, they won't be too hard on you."

The two girls glanced at the grandfather clock in the hall and then crossed to look at themselves in the mirror. Amy had slicked her hair down and parted it neatly on the side.

"You look nice," Palmer told her.

"Thanks," Amy said. "I wouldn't want your parents to think your roommate's a weirdo. I kind of did it for my parents, too," she confessed. "My dad hates unusual hair-dos almost as much as he hates rock music."

Amy patted her hair as the front door suddenly swung open, and Palmer turned to see her parents standing in the entrance. Her mother was bundled up in a long fur coat and her father's face was half hidden by a silky gray scarf.

"Hi, sweetheart," said Mrs. Durand, hurrying inside. "Sorry we're late!"

"Hi, Mommy," said Palmer, her throat tightening with emotion. It had been so long since she'd seen her family, and her mom was looking so beautiful.

"Hi, princess," said Mr. Durand, giving Palmer a hug.

"Hi, Daddy," she said, hugging him back.

"Look," Mrs. Durand said as she took off her coat, "we're both wearing pink dresses!"

"It's not just your dresses that are alike," Amy said, staring intently at Palmer's mother. "You and Palmer almost look like identical twins."

Palmer giggled. "Everybody says that." She took Amy's hand and smiled at her parents. "This is my roommate," she said proudly. "Amy Ho!"

"How do you do, Amy?" Mrs. Durand greeted her warmly.

"We've heard a lot about you," said Mr. Durand. "You're the one who wants to be a rock and roll star!"

Amy's face flushed. "Ah . . . not exactly," she said, glancing into the dining hall again.

"That's one subject we don't want to bring up at the dinner table, Daddy," Palmer said, hooking her arm through her father's. "Amy's parents don't like to talk about it."

"I see." Mr. Durand nodded. "One of those forbidden topics." He smiled at Amy. "Don't worry. I won't say a word about it."

Palmer and her parents walked into the dining hall with Amy. *So far, so good,* thought Palmer. Her parents seemed glad to see her, and they hadn't mentioned her grades yet. Maybe they'd forget all about them!

After the parents were all introduced to each other, the five-course dinner was served. Conversation came slowly at first between the girls and their parents. Even though Lisa, Shanon, Amy, and Palmer had become quite close at Alma, their parents hardly knew each other. Like their daughters, the adult McGreevys, Hos, Davises, and Durands were all quite different from one another. But the girls' high spirits and the excellent food helped break the ice. By the time the luscious strawberry shortcakes were brought out for des-

31

sert, the four families were chatting away like old friends.

After dinner, the girls gathered in the ladies' room.

"Isn't this terrific?" said Shanon. "I'm so glad our parents are all here."

"They seem to be getting along great," Lisa said brightly.

"Now, let's just hope that they get along as well with our pen pals," Amy said.

Palmer smiled and put on a touch of pale pink lipstick. That was one thing she didn't have to worry about! How could anyone not like Sam? Besides, her parents' mood was excellent—Palmer couldn't remember the last time she'd seen them so relaxed together!

"Here goes," Amy said, checking herself in the mirror again. "I hope John doesn't think I look like a dweeb in this dress and this hair!"

"Of course he won't," said Lisa. "Anyway, John's preppy, not punky."

The four girls left the ladies' room and met up with their parents in the hall. The families walked in a group toward the gymnasium, but halfway there the Durands began to drop back.

"Are you tired, Mommy?" Palmer asked, giving her mother a concerned look.

"No, dear," her mother replied. "I just thought we might talk a bit now."

"We're not too keen on going to this dance," Mr. Durand put in.

"But you have to go," Palmer cried. "My pen pal will be there. He's providing the music. His name is Sam and—"

"All right, all right," Palmer's mother said quietly. "We'll drop in for a bit, but then we have to go somewhere quiet where we can talk."

32

"We're leaving tomorrow morning, right after the conference with your advisor," Palmer's father explained. "We won't have time to—"

Palmer's stomach lurched. "You're leaving early? What about the rest of the weekend? There are all kinds of activities planned."

Palmer's father stopped in the middle of the path and turned to look at her. "The main reason we're here is because of your academic performance," he said.

"I know I didn't do great this semester," Palmer said hastily, "but I'm going to do better, you'll see."

"We'll talk about it later, darling," said Mrs. Durand. "Right now we need to get indoors. It's freezing out here."

Palmer trailed into the gym behind her parents. Lisa, Amy, Shanon, and their families had already gone inside and taken off their coats. Palmer was so upset, she hardly noticed the bright lights and decorations or the ONE HUNDRED YEARS OF THE LEDGER banner strung over the gym. But even across the crowded room she couldn't miss Sam and The Fantasy, onstage and playing her favorite song.

"That music is deafening," Mrs. Durand said, straining to be heard above the drums. "Not a bit like the dances in my day at Alma."

"Ardsley was pretty sedate then, too, compared to this!" Mr. Durand shouted.

Palmer moved closer to them. "I like the music!" she yelled in her father's ear.

Suddenly the band brought their number to a close and a moment of sudden silence descended on the room.

"Those drums," groaned Mr. Durand. "And Palmer's yelling in my ear didn't help."

33

"I'm sure I've lost my hearing, too," Mrs. Durand said, nodding.

"I think the drums are wonderful," Palmer said, two angry spots of pink coloring her cheeks. Her parents were criticizing Sam's music! They hadn't even *met* her pen pal, and already they didn't like him!

The band started up again, this time a little softer. Catching Sam's eye on the stage, Palmer smiled and waved at him.

"Who's that?" asked her mother.

"My pen pal, Sam O'Leary," Palmer said, blushing.

"Sorry, princess," her father said awkwardly, "I forgot you said he was providing the music. I didn't mean to make fun of him."

"Of course we didn't," her mother agreed. "Sam's the boy you wrote us about."

"Yes, the Ardie!" Mr. Durand said brightly.

"Well, he's *kind* of an Ardie," Palmer hedged. She'd almost forgotten that she'd called Sam an Ardie in her letter.

Mr. Durand chuckled. "If he's an Ardie, he's an Ardie all the way. Don't forget—I'm an Ardsley man myself!"

Just then Sam hopped down off the side of the stage and headed in Palmer's direction. The band continued to play a slow instrumental number without him.

"I saw you come in," he said, beaming at Palmer. Then he looked at her parents and blushed.

"This is Sam O'Leary," Palmer said eagerly.

"The Ardie!" Mr. Durand said, extending his hand.

Sam looked confused. "Excuse me . . . but I go to school in Brighton."

"He *used* to go to Ardsley," Palmer said weakly.

"Oh," said Mr. Durand. "I thought you said Sam went to Ardsley now."

Palmer quickly pulled Sam aside. "The band sounds great," she said, flustered.

"Thanks," Sam said. "You look a little strange. Is something wrong? How come your dad thought—"

"What number are you going to play next?" Palmer cut in quickly.

Sam flashed a smile. "It's a surprise for Amy."

"That's nice," said Palmer. "What kind of surprise?"

"Her pen pal John Adams arranged it," Sam explained. "I'm going to play one of her songs. Something called 'Stage Boy Blues.' "

"Gosh," said Palmer. "Does Amy know about this?"

"Nope," Sam said. "I told you, it's a surprise. John wanted Amy's parents to hear how talented she is."

Palmer glanced anxiously in her roommate's direction. Amy was standing with her parents and John. She wondered if there was time to warn her.

"See you later!" Sam said hurriedly. "I've got to go now. Amy's number is next!"

"Sam!" Palmer cried. "Wait!" But it was too late. Sam was already striding toward the stage.

Poor Amy, thought Palmer. What was her father going to say when he realized she was writing rock music? Looking around for her own parents, Palmer spotted them waiting in a corner. Instead of the relaxed smiles they had worn earlier, both her parents looked tense and irritated. Catching sight of Palmer, Mr. Durand lifted an eyebrow and tapped his watch. Palmer gulped. She had a feeling that time was running out!

CHAPTER SIX

Dear Palmer,

What happened to you the night of the dance? After I went up on stage to play Amy's number, you and your parents disappeared. You sort of looked sad—is something wrong? And why did your father think I was an Ardie?

Yours truly,
Sam

Dear Sam,

This is a hard letter to write. To answer your first question, my parents and I went back to Fox Hall because they wanted to talk to me in private about my grades. I guess I forgot to mention it to you, but I am on academic warning, which is pretty bad. Anyway, even my parents didn't know about that part. They found out the next day when they saw my advisor, Mr. Griffith, and boy were they mad! At first I thought they were going to pull me out of Alma, but they didn't. Instead they did something almost as bad—they cut off my allowance! I don't know what I am going to do now. I am used to buying whatever I need, and I need lots of things like clothing and hamburgers. I get so tired of dining hall food. I'm sure you will agree that this is a disgusting punishment.

To answer your other question, something I told my dad must have given him the idea that you were an Ardie. I don't know when I'll see you again. I have to spend all of my time studying and figuring out ways to get money. It is awful being broke.

Yours truly,
Palmer

Dear Palmer,
The thing about your academic warning is awful. You seem very smart to me. I am sorry about your allowance. Maybe you could do some kind of odd job, like baby-sitting. You said you wrote something to your father to make him think I was an Ardie. What was it that you said, exactly? I would really like to know. There is nothing wrong with going to Brighton.

Yours truly,
Sam

Dear Amy,
I don't understand what was going on with you the night of the dance at Alma. I liked your parents and thought we got along well. (Your mother is pretty.) But then when The Fantasy played "Stage Boy Blues," you seemed to get mad. Why wouldn't you dance with me anymore? And why did you leave in such a hurry?

Puzzled,
Your pen pal, John A.

Dear John,

How can you be puzzled? I told *you* not to have Sam play one of my songs and you went ahead and did it anyway. Not only that, "Stage Boy Blues" is horrible! I hadn't even finished working on it. It sounded awful when Sam and his band played it, and everyone heard it sounding that way. Now my father will never take me seriously as a musician. When he heard "Stage Boy Blues," he said that I was wasting my time. That if I really was serious about music, I should study it. My mother tried to be nicer about it, but I think you might have heard her when she said that my song was cute! My music is *not* cute—it is serious. But, thanks to you, my parents will never believe that.

Amy

Dear Amy,

Your latest letter left me flabbergasted. How can you be mad at me because your own father doesn't like it that you like rock music? Personally, I think "Stage Boy Blues" is a great song and something you should be proud of. Sam and The Fantasy did a good job with it, too. I asked them to play the number to surprise you, not to embarrass you. I also was trying to make you be more confident. I'm sorry that things backfired, but it is not my fault. My father never liked my poems, but I kept writing them anyway. He still doesn't like my poetry, but he respects the fact that I do! Besides, I read other people's poetry all the time, so he knows I am serious. Maybe you should find a way to let your father know that you're serious about your music, too.

Here's a new poem I just wrote. Thanks for the inspiration!

Stepped on by mistake
True to your nature, you are untrue
Eager to please everybody
And to be something eternal like a statue from Egypt
May I suggest, my lady, that you don't do it?
Evermore your friend, but at the moment steamed.
Don't write for a while!

Sincerely,
John Adams

P.S. Check out the acrostic.

Dear Shanon,

I really liked your dad. I thought it was funny when he asked me if I could change a tire. What did he think of me? I tried to dress normal. I also liked your mom. I bet she's a great cook. Write soon.

Mars

P.S. I liked your dress a lot, too.

Dear Mars,

My mother and father liked you, too, and since they live in Brighton maybe some weekend we could both get permission to leave campus and meet at my house for dinner. You're right—my mom is a fantastic cook, and so is my grandmother. You know something weird? I was afraid my father wouldn't get along with you or with the other fathers. He is definitely not the preppy type, and I thought he might think it was snobby, sitting in the big formal dining hall at Alma, especially with Palmer's parents. But he really had a good time. So did my mom, but she gets along with everybody. I wish you could meet the rest of my family. I have

39

fourteen cousins. Everybody should be as lucky as I am. Parents' Weekend was great. Lisa, Amy, and Palmer are glad it's over, but I'm not.

Love,
Shanon

P.S. How's your parrot?

Dear Shanon,

 Ricardo is fine, though he is molting a lot. Unfortunately, Rob seems to be allergic to his feathers, so he (Ricardo, not Rob) may have to go home to my folks next vacation. I have taught him (Ricardo) to say mucho frío, *which means "very cold" in Spanish. It is* very *cold here. Yesterday my hair froze after my shower.*

Love,
Mars

Dear Lisa,

 It was great seeing you at the dance. It was a good idea you girls had inviting us guys to meet your parents. Your father is a good man. He reminds me a little bit of my *dad. But the best thing of all was dancing with you. Hope this is not too corny.*

Love,
Rob

Dear Rob,

 Your letter was not too corny. My parents loved you! My father thought it was super that we write to each other. My mother said you were (get this!) "extremely cute." Of course, there's something really weird about my own mother calling one of my friends extremely cute, but I

40

thought I'd pass on the compliment. Exactly how tall are you now, if you don't mind my asking? My mother wanted to know. If you are interested, I am 5 feet 7 inches. I am glad we are both tall.

Yours,
Lisa

Dear Lisa,

I hope that if I was a short guy, you would still write me letters. But I am now 5 feet 9¼ inches. Yes, at fourteen I am a giant. And you are a giantess. Maybe we should try out for Jack and the Beanstalk.

I'm glad your mother didn't think I looked like Frankenstein. Your mother is cool. She looks just like you. I was amazed when I saw you together. Amy Ho's parents look like she does also, only Amy didn't look like herself that night. I hardly recognized her! Tell Amy she looks very normal with her hair combed that way.

I had a problem with my knee last week and I'm wearing a brace. In fact, I was wearing it at the dance, but you didn't know it. I hope my dancing wasn't bumpy. I was worried about that. I'd hate to be known as a bumpy dancer.

Your pen pal,
Rob

Dear Rob,

I can't believe you had a brace on your knee. I hope it isn't serious. Something you said in your letter sort of bothered me—the fact that you called me a giantess. I hope you don't really think I'm too tall. I am taller than most of my friends and most boys I know. But to answer your question, now that I know you, I am sure that even if you were short I *would like you anyway. I would certainly enjoy your letters. Height has nothing to do with writing. Write soon. I hope to see you again soon.*

Love,
Lisa

CHAPTER SEVEN

———◆———

"It's not fair!" Palmer sputtered, struggling to keep up with Amy on her ice skates. "I don't care if they are my parents. It's rotten!"

Amy slid to a neat halt. "Should we turn around or keep going?" she asked, breathing out a small cloud of white vapor. The two girls had skated the whole length of the frozen waterfront bordering the Alma campus.

Palmer squinted in the sunlight. "If we keep going, we'll slide right onto Ardsley's grounds."

Amy giggled. "Not a bad idea, but I guess Miss Pryn would find out sooner or later and we'd really be in trouble."

As they turned back and skated upriver, Amy glanced sideways at her roommate. "Don't get me wrong, Palmer," she said. "I think your situation is rough. I wouldn't know what to do without money either. But you have to admit you've been asking for it."

Palmer's face flamed. "Asking for it? Don't tell me you're on my parents' side!"

Amy shrugged. "Not exactly. But when they found out you were messing up in all your subjects, your mom and dad had to do something. At least they didn't transfer you from Alma."

"Thank goodness for that," said Palmer. "But they didn't have to cut off my allowance even after I promised to work harder in my subjects."

"You are working harder," Amy agreed. Only yesterday, Palmer had spent the whole afternoon in the library. And the night before she'd been up studying her history until lights out. "Maybe you should write a letter to your parents telling them how you're really trying," Amy said.

"It wouldn't do any good," Palmer sighed. "They don't take me seriously."

"I know what you mean on that score," muttered Amy, heading toward the boathouse, where they'd left their boots.

"You're talking about what your father said when he heard your song at the dance, aren't you?" Palmer asked sympathetically.

"I sure am," said Amy, plopping down on a bench and unlacing her skates. "My dad talked to me just like I was a little kid. He said rock was a nice hobby but a waste of time. And my mother called my music *cute!*"

Palmer winced as she pulled off her skates. "How embarrassing. Still, they probably didn't mean to hurt your feelings."

"They should have thought before they spoke," Amy said angrily. "Anyway, I'm sure they meant exactly what they said, especially Dad. My father thinks that in order to be serious about something you have to know everything in the whole world about it. I'd have to study music for a hundred million years before he'd ever believe I was serious about songwriting."

"And who wants to study *any*thing for a hundred million

years?" Palmer said glumly. "I wish I didn't have to study for even *one* hour!"

Palmer picked up her sparkling white skates by their pink laces, while Amy slung her own very used-looking black skates over one shoulder. Then, leaving the boathouse, they trudged up the snowy hill toward Alma Stephens.

"I'm also still mad at John, too," Amy said. "He should never have asked Sam to play 'Stage Boy Blues.'"

"My nose is frozen," said Palmer, looking up at the gray clouds above. "I just tried to wiggle it and I couldn't."

"Let's go to the snack bar for some hot chocolate," Amy suggested. "Or maybe," she added as an afterthought, "we could go to The Tuck Shop and see Shanon."

"No, let's go to the snack bar," Palmer said. "I don't want Shanon being a waitress for me. It's too embarrassing."

"I don't think she'd feel that way," said Amy.

Palmer shrugged. "Well, I would."

The two girls turned into Booth Hall and went straight to the snack bar. After ordering their hot chocolate, they took a table by the window.

"I'm hungry," Palmer said bitterly. "Right now I could eat three hamburgers. But with no allowance, I can't afford one! Thanks to my parents I'm going to starve to death."

Amy chuckled. "I don't think things will get that bad. It just means you'll have to take whatever's on the menu in the dining hall."

"Ugh," said Palmer, sipping her chocolate. "Creamed chipped beef, turkey goulash, shepherd's pie."

"Don't you like those gourmet delights?" teased Amy.

Palmer put down her cup. "You know I don't! And instead of helping me out, all you're doing is making fun of me. Do you realize this one cup of hot chocolate costs sixty

45

cents? I usually have two hot chocolates in the snack bar every day. Not to mention pie, hamburgers, banana splits, et cetera. Just keeping myself in hot chocolate would cost me over eight dollars a week!" Palmer continued. "And what about clothes? How am I going to get those suede boots I saw at Suzy's Shoe Emporium?"

"I guess the situation *is* serious," said Amy. "I could lend you money for extra food, but I don't know about the clothes."

"What am I going to do?" Palmer moaned.

Amy thought for a minute. "You could get a job," she offered.

"Sam suggested that, too," said Palmer. "But I just *couldn't* be a baby-sitter. Besides, all the baby-sitting jobs around here have been sewn up since the fall."

"There are other kinds of jobs," said Amy. "Maybe you could work in The Tuck Shop."

Palmer wrinkled her nose. "You mean be a waitress like Shanon?"

"Why not?" said Amy.

Palmer shook her head. "I'm sure it's too hard. Anyway, I'd be so embarrassed when kids I know come into the ice-cream parlor."

"Lots of people that Shanon knows come in there," Amy insisted. "And The Tuck Shop is perfect. It's a student-run business. It's just for the school."

"No thanks," said Palmer. "There's got to be another way. If only I had something to sell."

"That's easy. You've got loads of stuff. You have more clothes than Lisa, Shanon, and I put together," said Amy. She eyed the pastries near the cash register. "Want a donut?" she asked. "Don't worry about the money. It's on me."

"Thanks," Palmer said, brightening.

While Amy went to get the donuts, Palmer thought about all her possessions. She did have a very large wardrobe and tons of CDs and records. But they were all so special. At least she'd thought so when she bought them. It would be very hard figuring out which things she could bear to part with. Still . . .

"I think your idea is good," said Palmer when Amy got back. "We'll have a tag sale."

"*We?*" Amy said, chomping her donut.

"Well, I thought you might help me," said Palmer. "After all, it was your suggestion."

"Okay," said Amy, "I'll help—a little bit."

"Great," Palmer said. "My problems are over."

"Now, if only we could solve *my* problems," Amy said. "What do you think I should do about my parents?"

"What *can* you do?" said Palmer. "Parents are parents, and they have their own opinions about things. What difference does it make if your father doesn't think you're serious about music?"

"It makes a lot of difference," Amy protested. "I want my parents to trust me. I want them to at least listen when I say something's important to me."

Palmer's eyes lit up. "Hey, I have an idea. Remember how you said you'd have to study music a hundred million years before your father would believe you were taking it seriously?"

"Yes," said Amy. "So what?"

"So, why don't you?" said Palmer.

"Study music for a hundred million years?" Amy asked. "You've got to be kidding. Remember, I got thrown out of chorus."

"You didn't really get thrown out," Palmer reminded her.

47

"Professor Bernard just said that in order to stay in, you would have to learn to read music."

"Well, that's dumb," Amy exploded. "Lots of famous musicians don't know how to read music!"

"Maybe you're right," said Palmer. "But lots of famous musicians probably do. If you knew how to write notes, you could write down your songs so that other people could play them."

"That *would* be kind of neat," Amy admitted. "As it is now, when I invent a melody and I want to pass it on to somebody like John or Sam, I have to send them a tape or sing it to them myself."

Amy thought for a moment. "Actually, what I've always wanted to do," she confessed, "is to learn how to sing better. If I keep writing my own songs, I'll want to perform them."

"Well, then, that's the answer," said Palmer. "Start taking singing lessons with Professor Bernard. I hear he gives privates ones. Brenda Smith says he's great."

"Brenda and I don't always agree about things," Amy pointed out.

"You'll just have to find out for yourself, then," said Palmer. "Unless you don't really care what your parents think," she added nonchalantly.

Amy got up and began piling their cups and plates onto the tray. Palmer's idea made her nervous, even though she knew that taking lessons might just be the way to convince her father that she was serious about music.

"So, are you going to do it?" Palmer asked, slipping into her parka.

"Maybe," said Amy. "Maybe not. But thanks for the suggestion."

"Thanks for your suggestion," said Palmer. She flashed a

big smile. "Who would have thought that in one conversation we'd both find the answer to our problems?"

Amy chuckled. "What's the square root of sixty?"

Palmer's face fell. "What?"

Amy grinned. "That's one problem we still have to solve together. Remember, you asked me to help you with math this afternoon?"

"Right," Palmer said, smiling weakly. "I guess we'd better get it over with."

"To the library," Amy directed, pointing the way.

"The library?" groaned Palmer. "Can't we go back to the room? That way I can wash my hair first and go through my closet."

"That's exactly why we're not going back there," Amy said. "Do you want to pass that quiz on Tuesday or don't you?"

"I want to," Palmer replied earnestly. "Let's go study—and then we'll plan my tag sale!"

CHAPTER EIGHT

Curled up on the couch in the Fox Hall common room, Shanon stared at the blank page in her notebook. A gentle tap on the shoulder made her jump. She looked up into the violet eyes of the dorm's faculty resident, Maggie Grayson. "Problem?" the young French teacher asked kindly.

"I'm supposed to be writing something for the Centennial issue of *The Ledger*," Shanon explained. "The problem is, I'm stuck."

Miss Grayson sat down next to Shanon. "Maybe you should give it a rest," she suggested. "When is the article due?"

"Not for a while," said Shanon, wrinkling her brow, "but I hate leaving things until the last minute."

"I know." Miss Grayson smiled. "Why don't you go for a walk?"

Shanon shuddered. "Too cold."

"Then go listen to a record," Miss Grayson prodded. "I've been watching you. You've been studying extra hard these days, not to mention your new job at The Tuck Shop."

"I'm not at all tired," Shanon protested.

"That's not the point," insisted Miss Grayson. "Having fun is important, too."

Shanon shut her notebook. "Okay," she agreed. "I'll take a break."

Miss Grayson patted Shanon's knee. "That's a girl. By the way, I enjoyed meeting your folks. Your dad is certainly proud of you."

Shanon rolled her eyes. "He thinks I'm a genius. That's one reason I work so hard, I guess. I would hate to disappoint him."

"You're a smart girl, all right," Miss Grayson said, "and you've got plenty of motivation. You really don't have to try so hard, Shanon. From the look of things, I don't think you need to worry about disappointing your father."

Shanon smiled into Miss Grayson's eyes, then glanced at the small, sparkling diamond on the young teacher's finger. "Is, uh, you know, I mean . . ."

Miss Grayson laughed. "Are you trying to ask me about the wedding?"

Shanon blushed. "Yes, I know it's none of my business, but . . ."

"Of course it is," Miss Grayson said. "After all, Mr. Griffith—or shall I say *Dan*—and I are your teachers."

Shanon giggled. "I guess you know that we call you Dan and Maggie behind your back, huh?"

"Sure," Maggie replied, "and it's perfectly all right, as long as we're not in the classroom. But to answer your question about the wedding, the date hasn't been set yet. When Dan and I do decide, the girls in Fox Hall will be among the first to know."

"Thanks," Shanon said, smiling brightly.

A few minutes later Miss Grayson got up, and Shanon

51

was left feeling warm inside. There were days when Shanon missed her parents terribly, not to mention her sister Doreen and the others in her family, but having Miss Grayson living right in Fox Hall was a big help. Whenever Shanon felt lonely or had a problem, she knew just where to go.

Shanon shivered as the front door opened and a gust of cold air blew in.

"Hi," Lisa called.

Shanon took in the sprinkling of fresh snow on her roommate's blue hat and jacket. "Is it really snowing?" she asked eagerly.

"Started about fifteen minutes ago," Lisa said, stomping her boots on the doormat.

Shanon rushed to the window to see the swirling whiteness. "Fantastic," she sighed. "It's beautiful."

"Also wet," Lisa said, "and cold, but still beautiful." She shook off her snowy jacket and started upstairs. Shanon closed her book and hurried after her.

"So, what have you been doing?" asked Lisa.

"Working on my article," Shanon replied. "I gave up on writing something humorous. I told Kate and Dolores I couldn't do it. Now I'm just trying to imagine what things were like at Alma a hundred years ago. But I'm having a hard time with that, too."

"I have an idea," Lisa said, her dark eyes shining. "I think I know who can help you."

"Who?" said Shanon. "I've already asked Mars."

Lisa opened the door to Suite 3-D. "Mars wasn't a student at Alma a hundred years ago," she said mysteriously.

"And this person was?" Shanon asked in amazement.

Lisa laughed. "Not exactly. But my grandmother was an Alma girl. Gammy wasn't here a hundred years ago, but she was here fifty years ago."

"Wow," said Shanon. "That's amazing! I never would have thought of your grandmother."

"Neither would I until a few minutes ago," Lisa said, taking her boots off. She reached into the pocket of her flannel skirt and pulled out a letter. "Read this," she said.

Dear Lisa,

I am writing to wish you all the luck on the celebration of your school's Centennial. Here is twenty-five dollars. Please do something completely frivolous with it and think of your Gammy. In my day, twenty-five dollars would have been an immense fortune for a girl your age. I think I would have bought a hat with big feathers and several hundred sticks of hard candy from the sweet shop in Brighton.

Lots of love,
Gammy

P.S. I will be sending you a trunk of authentic nineteenth-century clothes. They belonged to my great aunt. They were just lying around in the attic. Hope you can put them to good use.

"Antique clothes!" exclaimed Shanon. "Your grandmother's so neat!"

Lisa nodded. "Not to mention generous. There's a sweater I want in the mall, and thanks to Gammy's twenty-five dollars, I'll be able to afford it."

Just as Shanon handed the letter back to Lisa, the door flew open. Palmer rushed into the suite, with Amy behind her.

"I'm glad you're here," Lisa said to Palmer. "Any chance you can sit for your portrait?"

"Not now," Palmer said, brushing past her. "Come on in here, Amy," she yelled. "We've got work to do."

"What's going on?" Shanon asked curiously.

"Palmer's going to have a fund-raiser," Amy said matter-of-factly.

"For what?" asked Shanon. "Some sort of charity?"

Amy chortled. "Not exactly."

Shanon and Lisa followed Amy into the bedroom she shared with Palmer. A stack of clothing was already piled up on Palmer's bed.

"Thinning out your wardrobe?" Lisa asked hopefully. "I could use those purple knickers on top if you don't want them."

Lisa reached for the pants.

"Not so fast!" said Palmer, blocking her way. "That will be twenty-five dollars."

"Twenty-five dollars!" Lisa exclaimed "No way! Purple's not even my favorite color."

"Okay," Palmer said quickly. "How about ten?"

"What is this," laughed Lisa, "a flea market?"

"Sort of," Palmer replied, pulling more clothes out of her closet.

Sitting down on her bed, Amy automatically reached for her guitar. "She's having a tag sale," she sang, purposely off-key.

Shanon looked shocked. "You're selling your *clothing*?"

"Why not?" Palmer said. "You're all always telling me I've got too much stuff."

"True," Lisa snickered, perching next to Amy on the bed. "But we never expected you to open your own boutique."

Amy struck a loud guitar chord and let out a snort. Even Shanon couldn't help giggling.

"Just a minute," said Palmer, her blue eyes flashing. "What's so funny?"

Lisa laughed and rolled into Amy.

"Hey, watch my guitar," Amy said, and she began laughing, too.

"It's just kind of unusual," Shanon said sheepishly.

"It's also unusual for me not to have an allowance anymore," Palmer said firmly. "Amy made a very good suggestion that I could get extra money by selling some of the clothes I don't wear anymore. And I'm going to take her up on it—no matter how funny you think it is."

Lisa sat up. "Actually, it's not such a bad idea," she admitted. "It just came as a surprise. And if you can't use all those great clothes, it's nice to give somebody else a chance to wear them."

"I think so, too," said Shanon. "Only . . ."

"I know just what you're going to say," Lisa prodded. "That nobody in this dorm could afford Palmer's prices."

Palmer sat down on a stack of sweaters. "Really?" she said.

"When people go to a tag sale," Lisa said wisely, "they expect a bargain. I would never buy those purple knickers for twenty-five or even ten dollars at a tag sale."

"Hmmm," said Palmer, "what would you pay for them?"

Lisa looked at her boldly. "Fifty cents."

"Fifty cents!" Palmer gasped. "That's ridiculous."

"That's all I can afford," Lisa said stubbornly.

Palmer took a deep breath. "Okay, then. Take them."

"Wow," Lisa said ecstatically, "thanks." She grabbed the pants and ran to her room. "I'll go get the fifty cents for you."

"Well, that was easy," Palmer said. "My first sale. I don't even think I'll mark the things. I'll just invite the whole dorm in and bargain with people."

Amy lifted an eyebrow. "Are you sure about that?"

"Maybe you should organize things first," Shanon suggested.

"That's okay," said Palmer. "I've got so much stuff here, that no matter what I charge I'll make a mint."

"If you say so," Amy said doubtfully.

"Of course," Palmer added, "I'm not going to be silly enough to sell anything else for just fifty cents. I only did that because Lisa's a friend."

"Not to mention a suitemate," Shanon said, hinting, "and one of the Foxes of the Third Dimension."

Palmer gave Shanon a knowing smile. "What are you getting at?"

"That cream-colored sweater," Shanon said, blushing.

"Sold for fifty cents!" Palmer said magnanimously.

Amy laughed. "Don't forget me. I'll take the brown leather belt."

"Not for fifty cents," Palmer said shrewdly.

"Okay," said Amy. "How about seventy-five, then?"

"It's yours," said Palmer, handing over the belt.

Just then Lisa appeared in Palmer's old purple knickers. "How's the sale going?" she asked cheerfully.

"If it keeps going like this," said Amy, "Palmer won't have any clothes, but she won't have any money either."

"Don't worry," Palmer said, bringing some skirts out of her closet. "I only let you have all those things cheap because I live with you. But not another thing is leaving this room for less than two dollars."

"Two dollars," said Shanon, "is still a bargain! I'm going to tell Kate. She could use some clothes."

"And I'll go knock on Brenda's door," Lisa volunteered. "She loves the way Palmer dresses."

"While you're at it, knock on everyone else's door," Palmer directed. "And stop by the dorm kitchen and grab some nachos. I put a stash under the sink."

"Right!" Lisa yelled excitedly, already out the door.

Amy and Palmer were left alone in the room. "Want me to help you?" Amy asked, softly strumming her guitar.

"That's okay," Palmer said brightly. "Just keep playing some music. That'll entertain the customers—that and the nachos."

"I get it." Amy grinned. "Just like the piped music in the malls and all the free little munchies they hand out in the grocery store."

"Correct," said Palmer. "Anyway, we might as well make it into a party." She stood back and surveyed her merchandise. Dozens of sweaters in assorted colors were stacked on the bed. Dresses of varying lengths and fabrics were draped over the bookcase. She'd even thrown in a hardly worn granny gown.

"Leave it to you to do something like this," Amy said with a giggle.

"You're the one who gave me the idea," Palmer protested.

Amy laughed. "And *you're* the one who's carrying it out," she said as the first group of customers began streaming into Suite 3-D.

Muffin Talbot, the shortest third-former in Fox Hall, made a beeline for a red silk blouse that was spread out on the bed. "What do you think?" she asked, marching up to Palmer. She held the blouse in front of her.

"It looks terrible," Palmer said bluntly. "It's at least two sizes too big for you."

"But I like the color," Muffin argued.

"She could always roll up the sleeves," Shanon suggested.

"No," Palmer said firmly, "I won't let you buy it, Muffin. It's too gross."

"Hey, Palmer," Amy whispered in her roommate's ear. "You're supposed to be *selling* stuff, remember?"

"Oh, right," said Palmer. "Next time, I'll sell something—no matter what it looks like on the person," she vowed just as Kate Majors strolled over in a fake-fur leopardskin pillbox hat that had once belonged to Palmer's mother.

"How does this look on me?" Kate asked Shanon earnestly.

"Well, it certainly is . . . interesting," Shanon said, trying to be diplomatic. "But I'm not sure it's really *you*," she added.

"She looks fabulous in it!" Palmer protested, elbowing Shanon out of the way.

Kate smiled doubtfully. "Do you think so? I was just trying it on for a joke. I'm not sure I—"

"It's really cool-looking," Palmer insisted, jutting her chin out. "It's my hat and I say that you look cool in it."

"Great," Kate said, setting the hat at an angle. "How much is it?"

"How much do you think it should be?" Palmer asked.

"I don't know," Kate replied. "Fifty cents?"

"Fifty cents!" Palmer cried. "You've got to be kidding!"

"It's fake fur," Kate argued.

"Okay," Palmer sighed. "You can have it for a dollar."

Amy sidled up next to her roommate. "How's it going?" she asked, offering Palmer some nachos.

"Horrible," Palmer sniffed. "Everybody here is a cheapskate."

"Maybe you should set the prices really high," Amy

suggested. "Then even if they bargain you down, you'll still get a decent price."

"Hey, Palmer!" squealed Lisa, running over. "I think I've made a sale for you. Germaine Rich says she'll pay ten dollars for your blue silk blouse!"

"That's not for sale!" Palmer exclaimed, heading toward Germaine. "And neither are those pink pants," she said, snatching them out of the girl's hand. "They were just lying out there!"

While Germaine tried to wheedle Palmer into making the sale, Lisa settled back on the bed with Amy and Shanon. "How do you think the sale is going?" she asked.

"I have no idea," Amy replied, "but it's sure turning out to be a good party." And with that, she turned up the volume on the CD player. Shanon went to the kitchen for some nachos, and the sale continued.

Standing in the middle of the room, Palmer was surrounded by clothes and confusion. She looked away as Gina Hawkins slipped on her favorite red skirt and Dolores Countee tried to squeeze into her favorite black boots. She could barely stand to watch Dawn Hubbard modeling her favorite yellow sweater. In fact, now that she was about to lose them, all of Palmer's clothes seemed to be favorites.

"How much is this skirt?" Gina clamored.

"I'll take these boots," Dolores trilled.

"What about this yellow sweater?" Dawn yelled.

Palmer began to sweat. "Gee, I don't know. Maybe I shouldn't sell—"

"Not sell?" squawked Dolores. "How can you not sell? This is a sale!"

"All right," Palmer said, gritting her teeth. "All items are the same price—seventy-five dollars!"

The girls burst out laughing.

"She's joking," Gina giggled.

"She has to be," Dolores agreed.

"Well, make me an offer," Palmer shouted over the din. Everybody started bargaining at once, but Amy had turned up the CD player so loud that Palmer could hardly hear.

"Okay! Okay!" she screamed. "Everybody just pay whatever you think the stuff is worth." And dropping a purple hat down near the door, she added, "Put your money in the hat before you leave. I'm going to get a soda."

"All *right*!" cheered Muffin, grabbing another blouse. "This is what I call a real sale! Hooray for Palmer!"

"How'd you do?" Amy asked, munching the last of the nachos. The tag sale was finally over, and everyone had left with their loot. Lisa and Shanon were studying at the library, and Palmer was sitting cross-legged on the sitting-room floor, counting her money.

"Thirty-five dollars," she said grimly. "Not much of a profit for just about my whole wardrobe."

Amy shook her head sympathetically. "You probably shouldn't have left the prices up to the customers."

Palmer sighed. "It seemed like a good idea at the time. I didn't think they'd all be so cheap. I guess I'm just not cut out to be a businesswoman."

"You were great," Amy encouraged her. "We just should have taken more time to organize things."

"Well, let's look on the bright side," Palmer said, perking up. "Thirty-five dollars won't buy much in the way of clothing, but it does translate well into hamburgers."

"What do you mean?" Amy asked.

"It'll buy me eleven point six burgers at the snack bar!" Palmer said proudly. "That's enough to keep me going for nearly two weeks."

"Great," Amy agreed. "You know, I've noticed one good thing that's been happening since you lost your allowance."

"What's that?" Palmer asked innocently.

Amy chuckled. "You're learning math!"

CHAPTER NINE

Amy took a deep breath outside the music studio. Behind the door, she knew, Professor Graham Bernard was waiting for her. Amy had seen him go in a few minutes earlier. *What am I doing here?* she thought, jamming her hands into the pockets of her short leather jacket. Ever since she could talk, Amy had been singing. When she was three years old and making up songs, her parents had been proud of her. But now they thought she was just wasting her time.

Amy stared at the closed door to the studio. From inside she could hear the faint tinkle of a piano. She pressed her ear to the glass. Professor Bernard was playing a song she'd never heard before. The melody sounded like something from a Broadway musical. She supposed she'd have to sing songs like that if she took voice lessons.

"Forget it," Amy muttered out loud. "I couldn't."

Just then the door opened and Professor Bernard appeared in the doorway. He was a towering figure with longish white hair and a bushy white beard. Behind his back, some of the girls jokingly called him Kringle.

"Miss Ho?" The professor's voice was deep and intimidating. "Don't we have an appointment? Or were you planning to stand outside the door forever?"

"You—you knew I was out here?" Amy stammered.

The professor tugged at his earlobe. "I have excellent ears, especially for someone over seventy. Besides, I saw you at the water fountain when I came in."

Amy blushed. "Oh, I'm sorry. I didn't see . . . uh, I didn't know you saw me. I saw you, too," she added hastily.

The professor's blue eyes seemed to peer right through her, but unlike his deep voice, his gaze wasn't at all frightening to Amy. In fact, she had never seen a pair of eyes more curious and twinkly. Maybe that was another reason why the girls called him Kringle—that and his white beard.

"Kindly step in," Professor Bernard said firmly, "or I'll leave you out in the hall and shut the door. There's a draft."

Amy darted into the room, and the professor reached over her head and shut the door behind them. The sight of the huge grand piano in the middle of the room was almost breathtaking. Amy's mouth dropped open as she admired the instrument.

Professor Bernard sat down on the piano bench and struck a mellow chord. "Let's begin on *A*, shall we?" He turned his head in Amy's direction and gave her a nod.

Suddenly Amy froze with panic. "I don't think I can," she blurted out. "I really can't sing. I just thought that if I took voice lessons, my parents wouldn't think I was goofing off when I wrote songs. But it's really a dumb idea. Now, I see that. You see, I can't sing," she repeated helplessly. "Not really."

Professor Bernard struck the chord more emphatically. "Nonsense," he said. "I had you in chorus."

"You kicked me out," Amy reminded him. "I couldn't read music."

Professor Bernard waved his long fingers. "That was ages ago. Since then, I heard you sing in the school musical."

Amy blushed. In Gina Hawkins's rock musical, she'd actually played the lead part. "That was just rock 'n' roll," she mumbled modestly. "The people who wrote the music for that show made it real easy when they found out I'd be singing it. I was yelling actually, not singing. Not real singing, like opera or anything. Besides," she added, "my voice is too deep."

"What's wrong with a deep voice?" Professor Bernard bellowed. "And how do you know *what* kind of voice you've got until you've learned to use it properly?"

Amy was left speechless.

The professor cocked his head and gave her a long, unblinking stare. "Now, enough excuses," he continued in a gentler voice. "Let's have our lesson, shall we? Let's have . . . fun!"

Shanon pulled off her white waitress apron and dried her hands on a dish towel. Another afternoon at The Tuck Shop was over.

"Here's your pay, Shanon," Mrs. Worth announced cheerfully. As supervisor of The Tuck Shop, the school dietician and cook handed out the weekly pay envelopes to the Alma girls who worked there. In fact, The Tuck Shop had been Mrs. Worth's brainstorm—the perfect way to teach girls home ec. and business management while giving them an opportunity to earn some money.

Shanon eagerly took her pay. "Thanks, Mrs. Worth," she said proudly.

The rosy-faced English cook beamed at her. "You're turning into a fine waitress, love," she said. "Pretty soon I'll have you running the place."

"Running The Tuck Shop?" Shanon exclaimed.

"That was the plan when we came up with this idea," Mrs. Worth explained, counting some tins on the shelf behind the small fountain.

"You mean the position of student manager?" Shanon asked eagerly.

"Hush," said Mrs. Worth, continuing her inventory of the stock. "I'll talk to you about it tomorrow. But now just you make a note that we're running low on chocolate syrup, and I'll also need more of that good strawberry."

"Sure thing," Shanon said, quickly entering the items on the list above the counter. She stuck her pay envelope in the zipper compartment of her knapsack and put on her coat. She wanted to know more about the student manager job, but she knew better than to interrupt the cook while she was doing inventory.

"See you on Tuesday," Shanon said.

"Right-o!" Mrs. Worth replied, not looking up.

Shanon dashed out the door into the cold, clear air. She needed some things at the drugstore, and Miss Grayson had offered to drive her there. Shanon spotted the teacher turning the corner in her bright blue car. Shanon ran toward the side entrance to meet her.

"Hop in," Miss Grayson said, pulling up at the curb.

"I really appreciate your taking me into town," Shanon said. "I'm running out of everything, even toothpaste."

Miss Grayson smiled. "No problem," she said. "I have to get some things there myself."

When they reached the Brighton Pharmacy, Shanon got out while Miss Grayson went to find a parking space. She quickly got her toothpaste and other toiletries. The money from The Tuck Shop would pay for everything she needed with lots left over. She stopped at a display of hair accessories and took a few minutes choosing a headband. Then she got a polka-dot ponytail tie for Lisa.

By the time Shanon had paid for her purchases, Miss Grayson was at the door waiting. "That was quick," she said. "Shall we go?"

Shanon smiled as she and her teacher got back in the car. She loved going to Brighton. It seemed so odd to be going to school just a few miles away from where her family lived and hardly ever seeing them. As Miss Grayson whizzed past the familiar stores on Main Street, Shanon suddenly felt homesick. If they made a right turn on Mulberry Lane, they'd be heading right toward her house. But in order to go to Alma Stephens, they had to keep going straight. When Miss Grayson drove past Mulberry Lane, Shanon looked wistfully out the window. She knew it wouldn't be right to ask Miss Grayson to stop. Her teacher was already doing her a favor by driving her in.

Shanon could easily imagine what her family would be doing right then. Her dad was probably still in the garage. But her mother would be getting dinner ready. Maybe she'd be cooking Shanon's favorite, spaghetti and meatballs. Shanon closed her eyes and sighed. Her mother's sauce was so incredible. She could almost taste it. Suddenly the car stopped. Shanon's eyes popped. They were parked in front of the local grocery store.

"Do you mind?" said Miss Grayson. "I'm out of tea bags."

"That's okay," Shanon said, hopping out. "I'd like to buy something here, too!"

Palmer gazed approvingly at the portrait. "Hey, that really looks a lot like me."

66

"I'm glad you think so," Lisa said. "I'd hate for you to hate it."

"The nose may be a jot too long," Palmer mentioned as an afterthought, "but other than that, it's fabulous. There's only one thing. . . ."

"What?" said Lisa.

"That scarf you've have me wearing is all wrong," Palmer said. "I look terrible in yellow. Do you think you could change the color to pink?"

"I don't know," Lisa said doubtfully.

Palmer ran into her room and ran right out again, trailing a long pink scarf. "Paint me in this, please," she begged. "I just got it. Isn't it beautiful?"

"It's great," Lisa admitted. "I'd better not touch it, though. I've got paint on my fingers."

"No, don't get paint on it," Palmer yelped. "It cost me seventeen dollars!"

"Seventeen dollars?" said Lisa. "Where did you get the money?"

"I made thirty-five on the tag sale," Palmer replied. "Don't you remember?"

Lisa shook her head. "I thought the idea was for you to get rid of your clothes so you could buy hamburgers."

Palmer sighed. "It was a good idea, until I realized I didn't have a stitch left in my closet after the sale."

"That's not true," Lisa protested. "You had loads of stuff."

"Not a pink scarf like this one," Palmer declared. "Anyway, I folded most of that stuff up and gave it away."

Lisa laughed. "Now, I've heard everything. You *gave* stuff away? To who?"

Palmer shrugged. "To the Brighton clothing drive. I saw

a sign when I went down to the public library for the tutoring project. I gave Mr. Griffith the boxes, and he dropped them off for me."

Lisa blinked in amazement. "Wow," she said, "that was really nice of you."

"Don't look so shocked," Palmer said, carefully arranging the new scarf around her neck. "Anybody would think you think I'm *not* a nice person."

"I don't think that at all," said Lisa sincerely. "Are we still on for our French study session this evening?"

"Still on," Palmer said. "Right after dinner. I don't know how people expect me to remember French grammar when I hardly know English. I got a D on my last spelling test!"

"Don't be so hard on yourself," Lisa said gently. "Everyone can see you're trying. I'm sure your grades will improve soon."

Palmer sighed. "Tell that to my parents."

"Have you heard from them lately?" Lisa asked, wiping her fingers on a paint rag.

Palmer shook her head.

"How about Sam?" Lisa asked.

Palmer's cheeks turned pink. "Actually, I owe him a letter," she said.

"Why don't you write one?" Lisa suggested, putting her paints away. "I'm writing Rob right after dinner."

"Maybe I will," Palmer murmured.

As soon as Lisa left the room, Palmer walked past the almost-finished portrait and sat down at the desk. More than anything, she wanted to write Sam a letter. But how could she without answering his question? Telling Sam that she had lied to her father, that she had told him Sam was an Ardie . . . It was all just too hard to explain.

68

CHAPTER TEN

—⚫—

Dear Mars,

   Have you ever been homesick? It's strange, isn't it? I was
so glad when I got my scholarship to Alma and my parents
thought I was ready to go even though I was only twelve
then. But sometimes it's really hard living here. Last month
I missed my sister Doreen's birthday. On our birthdays, my
mom always makes a big cake and we have a family party.
I guess I could have gotten a pass to go home, but I had a
big Latin test the next day. Of course I had to study for it.
Do you study a lot? I do. I take a lot of notes when I read
things. First I underline the book. Then sometimes I take a
second set of notes on my notes. Miss Grayson says I try too
hard, that I am very smart and have nothing to prove to
anyone. I hope she's right. Anyway, this letter was about
homesickness. When I started it, I felt really bad, but just
writing to you about how I feel has made me feel better. I
think I'll call my mom in the morning. Then in the evening
I'm going to do something very special. I'm making my
favorite meal for Lisa, Amy, and Palmer, only they don't
know it yet! Do you think that's weird—me making my own

favorite meal for everyone else? I got the idea this afternoon when I was in Brighton and I bought all the ingredients. I'm making spaghetti and meatballs in the dorm kitchen. Miss Grayson said I could. Do you like spaghetti and meatballs? My mom has a special sauce and I'm going to ask her for the whole recipe on the phone tomorrow. I wish you could be here to try my spaghetti. I'll let you know if it turns out okay.

Write soon.

Love,
Shanon

P.S. By the way, I really like my job. I wonder how long it will take till I'm sick of ice cream. A long time, I think!

Dear John,

I know you told me not to write for a while, but I just want you to know I'm sorry I got so mad at you about my song. I see now that you were only trying to do me a favor. I was never really mad at you, I think. I think I was mad at my parents, especially my father. He never seems to listen to me. He thinks he knows everything about me—more than I know about myself—but he doesn't. But how can I tell him that?

Today I had an amazing experience. I took a private voice lesson. It was hard. I was singing scales and weird combinations of notes. I didn't sing any songs. Of course, I know I don't have a great voice, but this teacher, Professor Bernard, doesn't mind teaching me, even though he threw me out of chorus because I couldn't read music. He made me sing some high notes. I was really shocked that I could sing them. It was weird. I didn't sound at all like myself. But I know one thing for sure—I love singing!

70

I hope you don't mind if we write to each other again.
                                          Sincerely,
                                          Amy

Dear Rob,
    I really miss you. Seeing you at the Ledger *dance seems like such a long time ago. I found a neat book in the library on the painter Van Gogh. He had a hard life. One of his paintings I liked especially is called* The Starry Night. *It's all dark with big splotches of light in it—beautiful and eerie. Palmer likes the portrait I am doing of her, but she wants me to make her look perfect. I can only paint what I see, though, and perfect things look fake to me. I mean, a fake apple is perfect but it doesn't look good to eat. Do you know what I mean? I can't wait until the Centennial Celebration weekend when I'll get to see you again. It seems like such a long time from now. What books are you reading? I just started* Wuthering Heights. *It's very romantic!*
                                          Love,
                                          Lisa

CHAPTER ELEVEN

"Passez-moi le beurre," Palmer said in a perfect French accent.

"Sure," Lisa said with her mouth full. She reached over Shanon's plate and passed Palmer the butter.

"Mmm," said Amy, scraping the last drop of sauce from her plate. "This is the best spaghetti I've ever eaten. I hope you made enough for seconds, Shanon."

Shanon waved toward the pot on the stove. She was enjoying her dish, too. "There's lots," she said between forkfuls.

Lisa sat back and sighed. "This was such a great idea. We should cook our own meals more often. Of course, none of us knows how to cook like Shanon does."

Amy giggled. "The only thing I know how to make is fortune cookies."

"Did your aunt in Taiwan send you the recipe?" Palmer asked.

"No," Amy replied with a grin. "My Australian friend, Evon, taught me, actually. She got the recipe out of a cookbook. Fortune cookies are fun, but they're not exactly traditional in Chinese homes. They're made for restaurants."

"It would be fun to make some, though," said Shanon, following Amy to the stove for seconds. "If you bake your own fortune cookies, it means you can write your own fortunes."

"That's just what Evon and I did," said Amy. "While the cookies were still hot and soft, we put the fortunes inside and then rolled them."

"Sounds like a lot of work to me," Palmer said, pushing her chair back from the table.

"Yes, but think what fun it would be to hand out cookies with your own fortunes to all your friends," Lisa said eagerly. "Now there's an idea for a business, Palmer. You could make a lot of money selling original fortune cookies."

"No thanks," said Palmer. "Baking cakes would be easier."

Lisa chuckled. "*You* know how to bake cakes?"

"As a matter of fact I do," Palmer huffed. "When I was in preschool, I took a cooking class."

"Wasn't that a long time ago?" teased Amy. "What kind of cakes were they? Mud cakes?"

"Very funny," Palmer said. "But it just so happens that cakes are very easy to make from a mix. The last time I was home, I made a devil's food one for my mother."

"Did she like it?" Amy asked incredulously.

"She was on a diet," Palmer admitted, "but my uncle gobbled it up. Thanks for the great supper, Shanon," she added, taking her plate to the sink. "Of course, now I'm so stuffed I don't think I'll be able to concentrate on my French. That vocabulary test is tomorrow."

"Relax," said Lisa. "I'll run through the list with you." She grabbed Palmer's French book off the counter. Palmer had brought it into the kitchen to study while Shanon cooked dinner.

"Hey, what's this?" Lisa asked, pulling a square white envelope out from between the pages.

Palmer snatched the book and letter from Lisa's hand. "Nothing," she said, turning away.

"It is too something," Lisa insisted playfully. "I saw the return address. It's a letter from Sam."

"From Sam, already?" said Amy. "Your letters must have crossed in the mail. It couldn't be an answer to the one you wrote yesterday."

Palmer's face flushed hotly. "I didn't write to him yesterday."

"Oh, I thought I saw you writing to Sam when I was writing to John," Amy said. She reached for Shanon's plate. "Finished with this?"

"Not yet," Shanon said. "I'm going for thirds."

Lisa grabbed an apron and started on the dishes. "You know what I'd like for dessert?" she said.

"What?" said Palmer, walking over innocently.

Lisa whirled around suddenly and snatched Palmer's letter away. "This!" she cried gleefully. "A nice juicy pen pal letter!"

"Hey!" Palmer cried. "Give that back to me!"

Lisa ran away and Palmer ran after her.

"Catch, Amy!" Lisa cried, tossing the envelope.

Amy and Palmer both lunged for the envelope, but Amy was quicker.

"She's going to tackle me!" Amy yelped. She thrust the letter at Shanon. "Here, Shanon, hide it! If she doesn't want us to read it, it must really be juicy!"

"*You* take it," Shanon giggled, passing the letter off to Lisa.

Palmer stood in the middle of the kitchen with her hands on her hips. "Stop it!" she screamed. "I'm not kidding!"

The other three girls stared at her in amazement. Palmer's face was bright red, and she looked as if she was about to burst into tears.

"Sorry," Lisa muttered. She glanced at Shanon and Amy, then handed the letter back to Palmer. "We were only teasing," she said sheepishly.

"We didn't mean to upset you," Shanon said.

Palmer sat down at the table and stared at the envelope. "It's no big deal," she said, "I might as well open it now. It can't be that bad."

"That a girl!" said Lisa. "Anyway, since when is there something bad about a letter from Sam?"

Palmer tore open the envelope while her three suitemates crowded around her.

"Hey, stand back!" snapped Palmer as she quickly scanned Sam's letter. "Give me some breathing space."

Dear Palmer,

How come you haven't written? All I'm asking for is an honest answer to a simple question: What did you say to make your father think I was an Ardie?

Sincerely,
Sam

"What's he talking about?" Lisa asked, puzzled.

"Something that happened at the mixer when our parents were here," Palmer replied.

"Well, what's the problem?" Amy asked. "Why don't you just answer his question?"

"I can't," Palmer blurted out. "He'll know I'm a liar."

"What do you mean?" asked Shanon.

75

"I told Dad that Sam went to Ardsley," Palmer confessed. "First I wrote it in a letter, and then I let him believe it at the mixer."

"Why did you do that?" asked Lisa.

"It just sort of happened," said Palmer. "I remembered that thing you said about 'once an Ardie, always an Ardie.' And since my parents are always finding something wrong with me, I thought if at least my boyfriend went to the same school as Dad they would like him and . . ." Her voice trailed off forlornly.

Shanon put her plate in the sink. "You really like Sam a lot, don't you?" she asked sympathetically.

Palmer nodded. "He's totally adorable—and a really nice person."

"Not only that," Lisa pointed out, "but you just called him your boyfriend."

Palmer's eyes widened. "I did? I guess I do think of him as more than a pen pal," she admitted.

"Then you'd better tell him the truth," Amy encouraged. "Sam *is* a nice guy. I'm sure he'll understand."

"Of course he will," said Lisa.

"I don't know," Palmer said unhappily.

"If you don't tell him the truth, you'll never be able to write to him again," said Amy. "Which is worse? Being honest or not having a pen pal."

"I guess you're right," said Palmer. "I'll write to Sam this evening."

"After we finish studying for French," Lisa reminded her.

The girls were almost finished with the dishes—Lisa washing and Amy drying—when Kate Majors stuck her head in. "Mmm," she sniffed, "I smell something great!"

"It's spaghetti and meatballs," Shanon said proudly. "I

made it. There's a smidge left in the pot if you want it."

Kate lifted an eyebrow. "You made it? Miss Grayson gave you permission to use the kitchen?"

"Yes, Kate," Lisa said sharply. "We have permission."

"Just checking," Kate said, strolling in.

Lisa got up to leave. "Come on, Palmer," she said. "Let's go."

"Just a minute," Kate called after them. "Don't forget to come to the bake sale next Saturday. I'm supposed to be spreading the word."

"That's right," said Shanon. "Everybody has to come. The proceeds are going to *The Ledger* fund."

"Gosh," said Lisa. "You already had that mixer. *The Ledger* must really be in trouble."

"We need a couple of new computers," said Kate. "It's nothing serious. Actually, *The Ledger* had a bake sale last year and it was really successful."

"How successful?" Palmer asked curiously.

"We made about two hundred dollars," Kate said, digging into the last of the spaghetti.

"Two hundred dollars!" Palmer exclaimed. "Can anyone do it?"

"Do what?" Kate asked, staring at her blankly. "Can anyone come to the bake sale? Of course."

"No," Palmer said impatiently, "can anyone *have* a bake sale . . . of their own?"

"I suppose so," said Kate, "if they get permission."

Lisa leaned inside the doorway. "You're *not* thinking of having a bake sale," she said, rolling her eyes.

"Why not?" Palmer said coolly. "It sounds like a pretty good deal. And I already told you—there's nothing to baking a cake."

Amy chuckled. "When are you going to do it?"

Palmer thought for a minute. "I know! There's an ice hockey match on Thursday! I'll make a bunch of cakes and sell them there at half-time!"

"Great," Amy said, "I'm not leaving until Saturday. This is one bake sale I don't want to miss!"

"What do you mean, *leaving*?" asked Shanon. "Where are you going?"

"I'm going home next weekend," said Amy. "Chinese New Year. My parents are—"

"First of all I'll need some cake mix," Palmer broke in. She jumped up and began rummaging through the cabinets. "Drats. There's nothing here but flour."

"Yes, cake mix is expensive," said Shanon. "It would be better if you made your cakes from scratch. That way you wouldn't eat up your profits."

"That's what I'll do," Palmer said decisively. "Although it's not as if I have to make two hundred dollars. I'll be happy if I can make fifty. I saw the most gorgeous plaid skirt at the mall, and that's how much it costs." She turned to Shanon. "Would you help me find an easy recipe for cakes? You're such a good cook."

"Sure," said Shanon. "I'll call my mom. But are you sure you want to do this? Baking a cake from scratch is an awful lot of work."

But Palmer wasn't listening. Full of spaghetti, meatballs, and her money-making plan, she went back to the suite with Lisa in tow as her French tutor. The only thing worrying her now was the letter to Sam. What could she possibly say to him? She felt dumb about lying in the first place. It was going to make her feel even worse to admit it to Sam. But she promised herself that before she went to bed, she would make things right. She liked Sam too much to keep on being dishonest.

Dear Sam,

This is a dumb letter and you are probably going to be mad. The reason why my father thought you were an Ardie is because I told him you were one. I'm very sorry. It doesn't have anything to do with what kind of person I think you are. I was just trying to think of something that my father would like. And since he went to Ardsley, I thought he would like you better if he thought you went there, too. I'm very sorry I lied. I didn't really mean to—it just kind of happened. Hope you are okay and that your studies are okay, too. I am having a hard French test tomorrow, but I really studied for it and am hoping to get a good grade.

Yours truly,
Palmer

CHAPTER TWELVE

Dear Shanon,

I was homesick once a long time ago when I was at sleepaway camp, but that was when I was nine. I wish I had been there to eat your spaghetti. I bet you're a good cook. I'm not a bad cook myself. Here is my own recipe for something sweet and yummy. You've heard of snowballs in winter. Well, these are mudballs.

Mars's Mudballs
One dozen chocolate candy bars
A bottle of maple syrup
A bag of popcorn.

Crush up the candy bars and put in a pot. Add maple syrup and cook over low heat. Stir in the popcorn. Make balls out of it. Mmm, good!

Try it, you'll like it,
Chef Mars

Dear Lisa,

I miss you, too. Maybe one day I'll figure out some way

of getting over there. Maybe even before the Centennial weekend.

Sincerely,
Rob

P.S. *I am not reading any books for fun unless you count comics or books for school.*

Dear Amy,
Thanks for writing to me. I'm the one who should be apologizing, though. I was trying to help you out with your parents, but I never should have butted in. If you mailed some of the poetry I sent you to my father without asking me, I'd be steamed, too. Your singing lessons sound interesting. Hope to bump into you one of these days.

Yours truly,
William Shakespeare
(only joking!—John)

"What a mess!" wailed Shanon, glancing around the dorm kitchen. It was the morning of the hockey match and Palmer's bake sale.

"We'll clean it up later," Palmer said, dipping her finger into a big bowl of batter.

"I'm afraid I've got to leave now," Shanon said helplessly. "I have a meeting at *The Ledger* office in ten minutes. If I'm late, Dolores makes me pay a quarter."

"What nerve!" exclaimed Palmer. "What good is a quarter anyway?"

"She puts it in *The Ledger* fund," Shanon explained. She looked at the messy kitchen again and then at Palmer. "Are you sure you'll be all right?" she asked.

"I'm great," Palmer replied cheerfully. "We've buttered

the pans and made the batter. All I have to do is pop the cakes into the oven."

"After you've beaten the batter," Shanon reminded her. She dropped a crumpled piece of paper onto the counter. "Here's Mom's recipe. Just follow the last few steps. I'm sure you'll be fine," Shanon added, dashing toward the door. "If I'm any later for *The Ledger* meeting, I'll be late for my job at The Tuck Shop."

"I hope you're not going to miss my bake sale," exclaimed Palmer.

"Don't worry. I'll be there," Shanon cried, already half-way down the corridor.

"Great," Palmer called after her, "because with all these cakes to sell, I'm definitely going to need help collecting the money."

With a satisfied smile, she surveyed the kitchen. "Piece of cake," she quipped, laughing at her own joke. Most of the work was already done. The girls had multiplied Mrs. Davis's recipe for chocolate cake by nine, and the rich batter lay waiting in three big bowls. On the counter near the stove were nine neatly buttered and floured cake tins. The oven was set at the right temperature—350 degrees. All Palmer had to do was pop the cakes in and wait. She was planning to bake them in batches of three. The recipe called for a baking time of one hour.

"So . . ." Palmer murmured, mentally calculating. "The whole thing should be done in three hours." Her smile broadened as she wiped her hands on her apron. She figured that there would be ten slices to each cake, which altogether would come to ninety slices! If she sold each one for fifty cents, she'd get forty-five dollars, just five dollars shy of the fifty she needed for the plaid skirt in the Brighton mall. With the ten dollars she had saved from her tag sale, she would have five left over for a cheap pair of earrings.

"Might as well get started," she told herself cheerfully. She glanced at the crumpled piece of scrap paper on which Shanon had scrawled her mother's recipe. The next step on the list was beating the batter. Palmer checked the cabinets for an electric mixer but couldn't find one. Instead, she grabbed a big wooden spoon. Though she'd never beaten a cake by hand herself, she'd seen her mother's cook in Florida do it.

Sticking the spoon into the first bowl, Palmer began whipping at the batter, but after only a minute or so her arm got tired. Beating a cake was hard work. She looked at the recipe. She wondered if there were any special instructions about beating by hand. Finding nothing like that on the front, she turned the paper over. But the only thing on the back was an old letter. It appeared to be something Shanon had written to Mars but never sent.

Palmer eagerly scanned Shanon's writing. A little voice inside told her she was being nosy, but another voice insisted Shanon wouldn't mind. After all, the four Foxes shared practically all their pen pal correspondence, at least the letters *from* the boys. The short note was pretty matter-of-fact. It was Shanon's invitation to Mars for the fund-raising mixer. Palmer thought it was pretty dull until she came to the P.S.—"Palmer did not invite her mom and dad to Parents' Weekend. I think she's kind of weird."

"*Weird!*" Palmer breathed aloud. "What's that supposed to mean?" Her eyes smarted with angry tears. All this time she'd thought Shanon was her friend. But it was obvious she wasn't. Palmer read the letter over again, and then again. . . .

Casting an eye toward the kitchen clock, Palmer was suddenly seized by a moment of panic. If she was going to bake and frost all nine cakes before the hockey game, she didn't have a moment to lose! With the words in Shanon's letter still burning behind her eyes, she grabbed the big wooden spoon and hastily started to stir.

When Amy left her singing lesson that afternoon, she felt like dancing! Professor Bernard made music seem so exciting. It was hard work learning to breathe the right way when you sing, and Amy's voice was still so underdeveloped that she could barely hit some of the notes Professor Bernard played on the piano. But all the same, after just a few lessons, it was clear that she was making progress. And today the professor had actually told her she had talent!

I have talent! Amy thought excitedly. Professor Bernard had said so. Someday she might even be a real singer. And if she kept learning about music, she'd be able to write any kind of songs she wanted to. For some time, she had noticed that most of her melodies were sort of similar. But now that she was being exposed to Professor Bernard, she was beginning to hear all kinds of music in her mind. Not only did the professor play an amazing variety of scales and combinations of notes in the voice exercises, but after each lesson he would jam awhile at the piano. At these moments the white-haired music teacher got pretty jazzy. As Amy entered the skating rink, her head was in the clouds and Professor Bernard's piano was ringing in her ears.

"Hey, Amy!"

At the sound of Palmer's call, Amy came back down to earth. Her roommate had set up a table for her bake sale right inside the entrance.

"You walked right by," Palmer complained as Amy backtracked toward her.

"Wow!" Amy said, taking in Palmer's goodies. "What are those?"

"They're cakes," Palmer said irritably. "What do you think they are?"

Amy started to giggle. The nine "cakes" crammed onto Palmer's tiny table were as flat as pancakes.

"Don't laugh!" Palmer snapped. "They're just a little flat."

"That icing looks thicker than the cakes. Whoever eats them will go into sugar shock," Amy said, still laughing.

"If you're going to make fun of me, go away," Palmer commanded. "Your laughing is bad for business."

"Sorry," said Amy, calming down a bit. "It's just that I've never seen cakes like these. Did you make them like that on purpose?"

Suddenly Shanon appeared out of a group of students that were drifting into the building. "Sorry I'm late," she said breathlessly. "I went to Fox Hall to help you carry the—" She broke off abruptly as she caught sight of Palmer's cakes. "What happened?" she asked in dismay.

"How do I know?" Palmer said angrily. She was still thinking about the P.S. on Shanon's letter to Mars. "It was your mother's recipe," she added, glaring.

"Mom's made this cake a thousand times," Shanon protested. "We must have left something out of the batter. But what? We were so careful with the measurements." She slipped off her jacket and dropped her books on the floor.

"Maybe you left out the yeast," Amy suggested. "That's what makes things rise, you know."

"The recipe didn't call for yeast—it called for baking powder," Shanon said. "And I know we put it in. We followed the recipe perfectly. Unless . . ." she said, eyeing Palmer, "you didn't beat the batter enough. How long did you use the electric mixer?"

"I couldn't find the mixer," said Palmer. "I beat the batter by hand."

"Gee," said Amy, sneaking some icing off the side of one cake, "you beat them by hand, huh? Pretty industrious."

"My arm almost fell off!" Palmer said proudly.

"You must not have beat them long enough," Shanon said. "Otherwise, they would have risen."

"How do you know how long I beat them?" Palmer grumbled. "Anyway, I don't need your help. I've got Amy."

"Shhh!" said Amy as Kate Majors and Dolores Countee strolled over. "Here come some customers!"

"My, my," Dolores said, shaking her head. "What are these—chocolate flapjacks?"

"No," Shanon said cheerfully, "they're brownies!"

"Palmer just baked them in round cakes because we didn't have any square pans," Shanon added with a big smile. "Want to buy one?"

"Sure," said Kate. "I love brownies."

"You'd better not," said Dolores. "Look how much frosting they have on them."

"Right," Kate said wistfully. "All that chocolate's not good for my skin."

"One won't hurt," Shanon tried to persuade her.

"No thanks," said Dolores, walking away and taking Kate with her. "Anyway, those are the strangest-looking brownies I've ever seen."

Palmer's face fell with disappointment.

"Don't give up," said Shanon. "We'll make a sale."

Suddenly Amy glanced toward the door and let out a gasp. "Oh, my gosh, look! There's Lisa—with Rob, John, and Mars!"

"What are they doing here?" Shanon said, blushing. "I mean . . . gee, I can't believe it! Mars is here."

Lisa and the boys walked over.

"Look who's here!" Lisa exclaimed with a grin.

"Thought we'd catch some of the hockey," Rob drawled, giving Lisa a long look with his dark blue eyes.

Lisa looked away. Rob's gaze was really intense! "Oh, what cute pies!" Lisa gushed, making small talk.

"They're brownies," Palmer corrected her.

Mars smiled at Shanon. "Did you make them?"

"No, uh, Palmer did," Shanon said, and felt her face flush.

Mars laughed. "They're kind of unusual-looking."

"I'll say they are," John chuckled. "They look more like mud pies than brownies."

"They have delicious ingredients in them," Shanon said, trying to rescue Palmer.

"It's Shanon's mother's recipe," Palmer declared.

Now it was Mars's turn to blush. "Sorry, I didn't mean to laugh at them." And turning to Shanon, he said, "I thought your mom was a good cook."

Shanon and Amy gave Palmer a helpless glance. Completely taken up by Rob, Lisa was paying no attention at all to Palmer.

"Does anybody want to buy one?" Palmer asked in a businesslike voice. "They're only seventy-five cents apiece."

"Sorry," John said good-naturedly. "I'm saving my money for popcorn."

"Hey, let's go inside," Mars said, touching Shanon's hand.

Shanon gave Palmer an apologetic smile before walking off with Mars. "See you later," she called over her shoulder. "I'll be back to help you, Palmer. I promise."

"So long, Palmer," Amy said.

"So long," Palmer muttered.

Deserted by her suitemates, Palmer stared at the nine flat "brownies." Her big bake sale was a big flop!

CHAPTER THIRTEEN

Dear Palmer,
I think that the way things have turned out, maybe it is a mistake for us to be pen pals. I think maybe we are too different in the things that we think are important. That means that I am probably not your type. Good luck in finding another pen pal.

Yours truly,
Sam O'Leary

Palmer read Sam's letter for the tenth time. He hadn't even mentioned her silly lie—or her sincere apology—but his message was clear. He didn't want to have anything more to do with her! And, Palmer thought sadly, she really couldn't blame him.

Sam had been a perfect pen pal. He had been interesting and different. That's why she'd liked him so much. Palmer was sure that no matter how many times she advertised in the newspaper, she'd never find another pen pal like Sam O'Leary. Why had she ever even thought to tell her father Sam went to Ardsley? Palmer liked Sam just the way he was. If only she had trusted her father to do the same.

Stretching out on her bed, Palmer pulled the quilt up to her chin. It was Saturday, and Amy was in New York for Chinese New Year. Lisa and Shanon had left the suite hours ago. Palmer laid her head on her pillow and started to cry. She cried so hard, she didn't even hear Shanon's knock on the door.

"Palmer?" Shanon sat down on the edge of the bed. "What's the matter?"

"Everything!" Palmer sniffed and wiped her tears away. "Go away," she whimpered. After what Shanon had written in her letter to Mars, Palmer wasn't about to confide in *her*.

"I can lend you some money," Shanon said softly. "I know you really wanted that skirt."

"I don't need any handouts from you," snapped Palmer, sitting up in bed.

"I'm sorry nobody bought your brownies. The boys shouldn't have made fun of them."

"They weren't brownies," Palmer huffed. "They were cakes. And why shouldn't people make fun of them, if they're flat? How was I supposed to know how long to beat them?"

"There was an electric beater in the kitchen," Shanon said. "I found it in the cabinet under the sink."

Palmer dragged herself out of bed and crossed to the mirror. "Too late now," she said.

"Did Sam finally write to you?" Shanon ventured, noticing the letter crumpled up on Palmer's bed.

"Go ahead and read it," Palmer said. "I guess the whole world will know sooner or later."

Shanon scanned the brief note. "Gee, that's too bad," she said.

"Yes, I guess Sam thinks I'm weird, too," Palmer said, facing Shanon. "Just like you do."

"I don't think you're weird," Shanon said.

"You do, too," Palmer countered. "I read that letter on the back of your mom's recipe!" Stalking over to the desk, she snatched up the batter-splotched paper and handed it to Shanon. Shanon gave the recipe a puzzled glance.

"Turn it over," Palmer commanded.

Shanon did what she was told and immediately recognized the old letter she'd written to Mars. "I—I didn't send this," she stammered. "I mean I decided not to say this. I mean . . ." At a loss for an explanation, Shanon felt her face turn crimson.

"So you think I'm weird," said Palmer, turning her back on Shanon. "Well, for your information, I don't care what you think. Everybody agrees with you, anyway."

Shanon got up and crossed to Palmer, who was now staring out the window.

"I'm sorry," Shanon said. "I did think it was weird of you not to invite your parents to the weekend. I write a lot of my feelings to Mars. And I almost wrote that one."

"But you *did* write it," Palmer pointed out, turning around again.

Shanon shook her head. "I know—and I wish I hadn't. But I never actually sent it. I didn't think it would be right to say something about you like that in a letter to anyone. It's not right to talk about your friends—even to another friend."

"Thanks," Palmer said softly. Her blue eyes welled up with fresh tears. "But it's the truth. I *am* weird. Everything I do is messed up."

"That isn't true," Shanon protested.

"Yes it is," sniffed Palmer. "I messed up in my studies and I messed up with my pen pal and I sold all my clothes for nothing at that dumb tag sale and—"

"And your cakes went flat," Shanon couldn't help adding with a smile. "You really have had a lot of bad luck. But we've had a lot of fun with you while you're having it."

"I guess the tag sale *was* sort of fun," Palmer had to admit.

"I enjoyed making the cakes with you, too," said Shanon. "And the fact that they were flat was my fault, too. I shouldn't have left you to finish them by yourself."

Palmer got a tissue and blew her nose. "You had someplace to go," she said. "Anyway, at least you got me started. I should have known the bake sale would flop. I guess I'm just a loser."

Shanon's hazel eyes widened incredulously. "You? A loser? The most beautiful girl in third form?"

"I am?" Palmer said, brightening.

"All the girls wish they looked like you," Shanon assured her. "And even if your parents cut you off for a while, they're bound to give you an allowance again someday. And I bet it'll be a big, fat one."

"Hmmph!" said Palmer. She crossed back to the bureau and picked up her hairbrush. "They probably will give me my allowance back. It would serve them right if I didn't want it anymore."

"What?" said Shanon.

"I'm mad at my parents!" Palmer said, turning around. "Why did they have to take away my allowance and that's all?"

"What else did you want them to do?" asked Shanon.

Palmer grew thoughtful. "It would have been nice if they'd called me up or something to see how I'm doing. They never call me, you know. It's because nothing I do is good enough."

"I'm sure that's not true," said Shanon.

Palmer shook her head emphatically. "I know what I'm

91

talking about. I'm not a brain like my stepsister. Anyway, my parents are always busy. They don't have time to waste on me."

Shanon lowered her eyes. "Maybe you should talk to them," she suggested quietly. "They probably don't even realize they've been hurting your feelings."

"I could never do that," Palmer said flatly. "Anyway, what am I supposed to say? That I think they hate me because I'm not smart?"

Shanon nodded. "If that's the way you feel," she said.

Palmer looked at her fingernails. "It's been on my mind a lot," she confessed. "And now that Sam isn't writing to me anymore, either . . ."

"Don't worry, Palmer," Shanon ventured awkwardly, "you've still got us . . . you know . . . your friends."

Palmer flashed a smile. "Yes, it's great to have friends. Even if one of them does think I'm a weirdo!"

Shanon laughed. "Sorry about that. But you have to admit, we are very different. I'm shy, you're outgoing. You're gorgeous. I'm okay-looking."

"I think you're great-looking," Palmer cut in. "And being shy isn't such a bad thing. My dad once said he wished I was a television so he could turn me off for a while!"

"Gosh," Shanon said, "does your father joke a lot, too? Maybe he and my dad have something in common after all."

Palmer shook her head. "No way. Your parents and mine are even more different than the two of us."

"How can you be so sure?" asked Shanon.

"Your parents still live together," Palmer said, trying to sound matter-of-fact about it. "Mine don't."

"That must be hard on you," Shanon said sympathetically.

"I'm used to it," said Palmer. "Most of the time."

Shanon got up and fluffed Palmer's pillow. She wanted to do or say something that would cheer her friend up. But she couldn't think of anything. Unless . . .

"Guess what?" Shanon said. "I got a promotion today. I'm the new student manager of The Tuck Shop."

"Congratulations," said Palmer. She stared at Shanon for a moment. "You're really on the ball," she said finally. "You've got everything together."

"Not everything," Shanon said, feeling embarrassed. "My skin could definitely use some improvement. Look at this pimple on my cheek."

Palmer laughed. "Don't worry. It hardly shows. And it's probably just from eating all my leftover chocolate cakes."

Shanon picked up a bottle of Palmer's nail polish from the dresser and fiddled with it. She had an idea, but she wasn't quite sure what Palmer would think of it.

"So," Palmer sighed, pulling her hair back. "I'm in the same boat I was in before the bake sale—bankrupt!"

"I think I can help you out," Shanon said, cocking her head. "I have a proposition for you."

"No more sales, thanks," said Palmer. "I'm a flop at them. I'll just have to wait for my parents to come around."

"Not if you get a job," Shanon said.

Palmer stared. "A real job? Like yours?"

"Not *my* job," Shanon said. "I'm the manager now. But now that I've been promoted, Mrs. Butter is looking for a new student waitress."

"I don't know," Palmer said doubtfully. "I can't really see myself as a waitress. It's so . . . so . . ."

"Well paying?" Shanon supplied with a smile. "The Tuck Shop waitresses earn five dollars an hour."

"Five dollars!" Palmer exclaimed, suddenly interested. "That *is* good pay. I could make twenty dollars every week."

"Yes, you could," Shanon said encouragingly. "What do you say? Would you like me to recommend you to Mrs. Butter?"

"I don't know," Palmer repeated. "I've never done anything like waitressing. Is it hard?"

"I could help you learn the ropes," Shanon offered. "It's so much fun!"

"You actually enjoy it?" Palmer asked incredulously.

"Sure I do," Shanon replied.

"Wow," Palmer murmured. "And all this time I was feeling sorry for you. I thought you must hate having to work."

"It's fun to make your own money," Shanon said, jingling some change in her pocket.

"Yes," Palmer agreed, "especially if you're poor...."

"Like we are," Shanon said, grinning. "But there's more to it than money," she added.

"You mean ice cream?" Palmer asked, her blue eyes beaming. "Do I get as much as I want for free?"

Shanon laughed. "As much as you want. But I'm warning you—you'll get sick of it."

"Never!" Palmer protested. "I love ice cream more than hamburgers!"

"So, have we got a deal?" Shanon asked. "It would be great to be working together at The Tuck Shop."

"Why not?" Palmer said. "Only, I don't want to wear white sneakers with my uniform. Okay?"

"Deal," Shanon said. "That is, if Mrs. Butter hires you."

Palmer swooped her hair up into a ponytail. "Wow!" she said. "Wait until Amy hears this!"

"She'll love it," Shanon agreed. "I can't wait till she gets back from her weekend down in New York."

"Who gets back?" Lisa asked, carefully pushing the bed-

94

room door open with her shoulder. Her hands were splattered with paint and there was a pink splotch on her nose.

"Amy," Palmer replied, hastily moving her white silk blouse out of Lisa's way.

"I finished the portrait," Lisa announced.

"The portrait of me?" said Palmer.

"You should see it!" Lisa exclaimed. "You're beautiful!"

"Really?" said Palmer. "I hope you changed my nose. It shouldn't be too turned up. And I hope my eyebrows aren't too thick."

"It's perfect," Lisa assured her. "Your nose and your eyebrows and everything. I even changed the color of the scarf to pink. Everybody in the art studio thought it was exceptional! In fact, it's going to be exhibited in the art show during Centennial Weekend!"

"That's great!" said Shanon.

"I hope so," Palmer said nervously. "I don't want people looking at my portrait and not liking it."

"Let me worry about that," said Lisa. "I'm the artist."

"Well, let's go," Shanon urged. "I want to see this work of art!"

"Me, too," said Palmer, fluffing out her hair. "But first I have to change my clothes."

"Oh, no," Lisa groaned. "That'll take hours."

"It'll only take a minute," Palmer said, grabbing a blue plaid dress out of her closet. "I want to look just right."

Lisa lifted her eyebrows. "We're just going over to the art studio. Nobody will even be there."

"The art studio isn't the only place I'm going," Palmer announced, changing her boots. "After that I'm going to The Tuck Shop." She turned and smiled at Shanon. "I'm going to get a job!"

CHAPTER FOURTEEN

Dear John,

 I am writing you from New York where I'm visiting my family. We're having a wonderful New Year. Wish you were here. Surprise—my folks are being really nice to me about my music. My dad is very interested in my lessons with Professor Bernard. It's so good to be home. Hope to see you back at Alma for the Centennial Weekend celebration.

Yours,
Amy

Dear Rob,

 Don't forget Centennial Weekend! We'll be hanging around, but there will be lots to do. One thing is the student art show. My portrait of Palmer will be hanging there. I'm kind of nervous but excited. Hope to see you.

Love,
Lisa

Dear Mars,

Guess what? I got promoted to manager of the The Tuck Shop! When you come for Centennial Weekend, I hope I can take you there for a banana split. I got Palmer Durand a job there, too, and I am teaching her how to be a waitress. Also that weekend, we can stop by The Ledger office where Kate and Dolores are setting up an exhibition of one hundred years of The Ledger. The telephone interview I had with Lisa's grandmother was sensational. I think my story is going to be good.

See you soon,
Shanon

Dear Sam,

If you really feel the way you do about not being my pen pal, I guess this is my last letter to you. I'm very sorry it turned out this way.

Palmer Durand
P.S. Remember what you said when my parents cut off my allowance—that I should get a job? Well, I did, and it's lots of fun.

Dear Mom,

I got a C plus in my last Latin test. I also got a job in The Tuck Shop. I am sorry that I am such a disappointment to you. Please call me up or write to me sometime if you are not too busy.

Love,
Your daughter,
Palmer

Dear Daddy,

My grades are improving. My suitemates have been helping me out and I really am trying hard. Sorry I didn't turn out as smart as Georgette. I got a job in the student Tuck Shop, which is an ice-cream parlor. How are you? I am fine. I miss when we all lived together (just you, me, and Mom, I mean).

Love,
Your daughter,
Palmer

CHAPTER FIFTEEN

Palmer attacked a big tub of rock-hard chocolate ice cream with her scoop. It was her second day at The Tuck Shop and the first on her own without Shanon. Though she'd managed to get this far without spilling or breaking anything, she was still having trouble keeping up with the orders and remembering exactly what ingredients went into each of the concoctions on The Tuck Shop's long and elaborate menu.

"Chocolate cow . . ." she murmured out loud. "That's root beer syrup, chocolate ice cream, whipped cream. . . ." She rushed to the front of the shop, where her customer was waiting.

"One chocolate cow," Palmer said, blowing a wisp of hair out of her face as she set the glass down in front of Gina Hawkins.

"Sorry," Gina said, pushing it back toward Palmer. "You forgot the chocolate sprinkles."

"Sprinkles?" exclaimed Palmer. She glanced around at the busy shop. She was already behind in her orders. "Chocolate cows have sprinkles?"

"They do at The Tuck Shop," Gina said firmly.

Palmer swallowed and forced a smile. "Chocolate sprinkles coming right up," she said politely.

Dashing back to the fountain, Palmer passed Germaine Rich's table. She hadn't seen the snobbish upper-former come in.

"Don't tell me *you're* waiting on tables!" Germaine exclaimed loudly.

Palmer blushed and stopped short. "I'm, uh, just helping out my friend Shanon," she stammered. "She's the manager here, and she's, uh, sick today."

"How odd," Germaine said snidely. "I just bumped into Shanon Davis, and she looked perfectly healthy to me. And you," she added, running her eyes over Palmer's uniform, "look more like a waitress than a manager."

"It's just for the time being," Palmer said, pushing by. "Excuse me, please. I have to get some sprinkles now."

"And while you're at it," Germaine called out, "make me a banana split. A double!"

Palmer slid behind the counter to repair the chocolate cow. There were some things about being a waitress that she really hated. Like getting an order wrong or having a snob like Germaine treat her like a real servant.

The other waitress on duty slid in behind the counter. Her name was Megan and she seemed totally at ease in the busy shop. "How are things going, Palmer?" she asked.

"Okay, I guess," Palmer said.

Megan smiled and moved out. "If you need help," she said, "just let me know."

As Palmer served Gina her "cow," Brenda Smith walked in with two boys. Since it was the Centennial Weekend, the girls could have guests.

"Hi," Brenda said with a smile. "Just get us three chocolate malts."

"Okay," Palmer said, glad to see a friendly face.

"Where's my banana split?" Germaine called out.

"You'll have to wait for your malts," Palmer told Brenda, getting flustered.

"No problem," Brenda said as she and the boys took their seats.

"Hey, haven't I seen you somewhere before?" one of the boys chortled. "Aren't you a famous model?"

Palmer gave the boy a puzzled look.

"Don't tease her, Rick," Brenda said. "We just came back from the student art show," she explained to Palmer. "We saw the portrait Lisa McGreevy did of you."

"Awesome painting," the second boy added.

"Thanks a lot," Palmer said, batting her eyes. She wanted to sit down at the table and talk for a minute.

"You'd better get a move on, Palmer," Megan warned, whizzing past with a tray. "Mrs. Worth has her eye on you."

"Got to run," Palmer said to Brenda. And as she dashed past Germaine, she muttered, "I know . . . a banana split."

Scurrying back toward the counter, she almost ran into Mrs. Worth. The roly-poly dietician had come in only a minute ago. "How's it going, love?" she asked, taking in Palmer's flushed face.

"Great," Palmer sang out, grabbing a banana for Germaine's banana split.

"If you have any trouble," Mrs. Worth said kindly, "just ask Megan. She'll help you out."

"Don't worry, Mrs. Butter, oops! I mean Mrs. Worth," Palmer said firmly. "I know what I'm doing."

"Jolly good," said the cook, sailing away. "Keep up the good work."

The morning wore on. While Palmer made trip after trip behind the fountain to make floats, sundaes, splits, and malteds. She thought enviously of her friends. Shanon, she knew, was at *The Ledger* office, setting up the hundred-year-exhibition with Kate and Dolores. Shanon's telephone interview with Lisa's grandmother had been a huge success, and it was the main feature in the Centennial issue. Lisa, meanwhile, was at the art exhibition, showing her painting. On her way to The Tuck Shop that morning, Palmer had seen it herself. Even she had to admit that the portrait was wonderful. Lisa had not only made her look beautiful, she'd made her look smart! Palmer wasn't exactly sure she looked that way in real life, but it made her feel good to know that Lisa obviously did.

Glancing up at the clock, Palmer realized that by now Lisa had probably left the art show and was with Rob Williams. Rob and the other Ardsley boys had all been invited to the Centennial festivities. Shanon would see Mars. And after her lesson with Professor Bernard, Amy had arranged to meet John Adams. Then they were all going skating. For an instant Sam O'Leary's face flashed across Palmer's mind. If only he were here today, too, she thought wistfully. But when she thought about his last letter to her and the one she'd written back to him, she decided that Sam O'Leary was the last person on earth she wanted to see.

Looking up from a tub of strawberry ice cream, Palmer saw Mr. Griffith and Miss Grayson walk in. She walked reluctantly over to their table, her eyes on the floor. She wondered what the two teachers thought about her, now that she was on academic warning.

"Nice to see you, Palmer," Mr. Griffith said.

"You look wonderful in that uniform," said Miss Grayson.

"Thanks," Palmer mumbled, sneaking a look at them.

Mr. Griffith ordered a butterscotch sundae and Miss Grayson a strawberry soda. Palmer put extra whipped cream on both of them.

When she placed their orders on the table, the two teachers were smiling warmly.

"Your last French test was a real improvement," Miss Grayson volunteered. "I can tell you've really been studying."

"I have," Palmer said proudly.

"You've made real progress," Mr. Griffith said, dipping into his dessert. "Not only that," he added with a grin, "but you make a terrific butterscotch sundae!"

Palmer grinned back before marching off to wait on the next table.

"Where are they?" Lisa said, stamping her feet nervously.

"Mars said he'd be here," Shanon said. "He's never broken a promise."

"They're probably having a snowball fight," reasoned Amy.

The three suitemates were standing outside Thurber Hall, dressed in their snow parkas. Underneath, they had carefully chosen outfits. Shanon was wearing an ankle-length green skirt, striped turtleneck, and the shiny brown boots she'd bought with her Tuck Shop earnings. In her pierced ears, she wore turtle-shaped earrings made out of origami paper. Lisa's earrings were also unusual—a series of dangling gold hoops with crimson beads almost the same deep red as her sweater and leggings. Under her parka Amy had on a black jumpsuit. And on her head she wore a leather helmet that made her look like an aviator.

"It's taking them so long to get here," Lisa grumbled,

103

blowing on her fingers. "Maybe we shouldn't go skating."

"Maybe not," Shanon agreed, eyeing their pile of ice skates. "What I could really go for now is some hot chocolate."

But just then, Lisa caught sight of their pen pals. The boys were running up the path, hurling snowballs at each other.

"Just like you said, Amy," Lisa giggled. "They're having a snowball fight."

Suddenly the snowballs were flying in Amy, Shanon, and Lisa's direction.

"Surprise attack!" Rob shouted, running toward Lisa.

"No fair!" Lisa shrieked, grabbing some snow. "We weren't prepared!"

Mars and John ran up to Shanon and Amy.

"What's cooking, good-looking?" Mars quipped.

"Not much," Shanon said with a grin. "Wait," she added, suddenly flustered. "What am I talking about? There's a lot cooking here today. It's the Centennial!"

"Mars sends Shanon out of orbit," John joked, giving Amy a nudge.

"Yeah," Rob boasted, "we guys have that effect on people."

The girls giggled and the boys laughed awkwardly.

"Hey, you forgot your skates," Amy said to John.

"We sort of thought we'd skip the skating," John explained.

Rob shuffled. "We sort of wanted to check out the art show."

Mars cleared his throat and turned to Shanon. "Listen," he said, "we have to ask you girls a favor. You see, we—"

"Please ask," Lisa broke in. "I'm freezing."

"Maybe we should go inside," Amy suggested.

"No, wait!" said Rob with a quick glance down the snowy path toward the parking lot.

John stepped forward. "We got a ride here from the coach, and we picked up a friend of ours in town. He wasn't exactly invited, though."

"Who is it?" Lisa asked curiously.

"Hey, buddy!" Mars yelled. "Come on up here!"

Sam O'Leary peeked out from behind a tree, then started walking toward them.

"I don't get it," Amy said to John. "How come Sam's here?"

"Palmer and Sam aren't pen pals anymore," Lisa put in.

"We know," said John, "but Sam wanted to come anyway."

"If Palmer had wanted Sam to be here, she would have invited him herself," Lisa insisted.

Sam walked up to the group. "Hi, everybody," he said. There was a moment of silence. "I, uh, hear Palmer's picture is at an art show."

"Yes, it is," Lisa said cautiously.

"I told him about your painting," Rob explained.

"Uh, well," Sam said, obviously embarrassed. "I just thought I'd say hi to everyone. See you later."

"Wait a minute, Sam," Shanon finally spoke up. She pulled Lisa and Amy into a huddle.

"He shouldn't be here!" Lisa whispered. "Palmer doesn't like him anymore."

"That's not true," said Shanon. "She thinks *he* doesn't like *her*."

"The least we could do is show him Palmer's portrait," Amy suggested. "What harm could that do?"

105

"What's it going to be, Foxes?" Rob asked, ambling over. "Does our buddy get an invite or not?"

The three girls looked at each other and then glanced over at Palmer's ex–pen pal. "Okay," Lisa said. "Hey, Sam," she called. "Want to come to the art show with us?"

"Sure," Sam said. "I hope you don't get the idea that I'm looking to bump into Palmer, though."

"We don't get that idea," said Amy. "You just want to see the portrait, right?"

"Right," said Sam. "Just the painting."

"Negotiations are over," Rob announced, grabbing Lisa by the arm. "Let's go see some art!"

As soon as they entered the gallery, Lisa led Sam and the others straight to her painting. Sam stared at it for a long time.

"It's going to disintegrate if you look at it any longer, O'Leary," John teased.

"I bet he'd rather see the real girl," Mars piped up.

"Lay off," Sam said irritably.

Amy motioned Shanon and Lisa aside. "I've got a great idea," she said. "Let's take Sam to The Tuck Shop!"

"You think we should?" said Shanon.

"Why not?" said Amy. "Mars is right. Sam obviously wants to see Palmer, and I'm sure it would make her happy to see him."

"If Palmer and Sam saw each other now, they'd probably make up and become pen pals again," Lisa agreed.

"Wouldn't that be great!" Shanon exclaimed.

With Rob, John, Mars, and Sam in tow, the three girls set off for The Tuck Shop. They had just settled down at a center table when Palmer came out of the kitchen. She was carrying a big tray loaded down with sundaes and sodas.

106

Catching sight of Sam with her suitemates and their pen pals, she stopped dead in her tracks. Shanon instantly got up and came over.

"What's going on?" Palmer choked. The heavy tray in her hands was beginning to shake. "What's *he* doing here?"

Before Shanon could answer, Sam began to rise from his seat. Not knowing what to do, Palmer backed up with the tray—and bumped smack into Megan, who was coming around the side of the fountain.

"Excuse me," Palmer muttered, trying to escape. Dodging Megan, she knocked over a stool and lost her balance. Before she knew what was happening, the tray and all the ice-cream dishes went flying. For a long, silent moment, Palmer just stood there, watching in horror as a red-faced Sam began mopping ice cream and syrup off his blue jeans. Then she turned on her heel and fled back to the kitchen.

"Are you okay?" Shanon cried, running after her.

"What do you think?" Palmer replied. Hot tears streamed down her face. "If this is your idea of a joke, it's not very funny."

"It's not a joke," Shanon protested. "Sam just wanted to . . . I mean, we decided that . . ."

"Don't even try to explain," hissed Palmer. "First Sam finds out I'm a liar, then he dumps me, and then he comes to make fun of what a bad waitress I am!"

"But you're not a bad waitress," Shanon argued. "You only dropped the tray because you were upset. It could have happened to anyone."

"I wouldn't have dropped it if Sam hadn't been spying on me," Palmer said angrily. "Why did you have to bring him here?"

Shanon hung her head. "I'm sorry. We were only trying

to help." She glanced out of the kitchen into the shop. "He's gone now anyway," she said softly.

Palmer's blue eyes filled with new tears. "Sam's gone?" she said. "He didn't even say hello to me."

"He must have been too embarrassed," said Shanon. "I guess it wasn't such a good idea to bring him."

Palmer sighed. "You can say that again!"

CHAPTER SIXTEEN

One week later, Lisa, Amy, and Shanon were sitting in their suite drinking hot chocolate. They were all wearing old-fashioned long skirts, lacy white blouses, and floppy hats.

"It sure was nice of your grandmother to send us these old clothes," Shanon sighed, snuggling into the loveseat.

"They were just lying around in the attic," Lisa explained, rummaging around in her grandmother's trunk, "so Gammy thought we might as well get some fun out of them."

Amy adjusted the big, feathered hat she was wearing. "Kind of a change from my usual wardrobe," she giggled.

"Hey, look at this!" Lisa exclaimed, pulling out a parasol.

"We should save that for Palmer," said Amy.

"I think she'd look great in this, too," Lisa said, holding up a frilly petticoat.

Shanon smiled dreamily. "Things certainly must have been different in the old days at Alma."

Amy nodded. "Sounds that way in the interview you did with Lisa's grandmother." She picked up the Centennial issue of *The Ledger* and turned to Shanon's article. "It says here that in the old days, the girls kept their musical instruments in their rooms."

"Just like you keep your guitar and your dulcimer," Lisa pointed out.

"But Shanon's article says that your grandmother kept a harp in her room!" Amy exclaimed. "That's a little bit bigger than a guitar."

"Not only that," Shanon added, "but her roommate had her own piano!"

"Now that's an idea," Amy said eagerly. "Since I started taking lessons with Professor Bernard, I've been thinking about learning to play the piano, too."

"Forget it!" said Lisa. "If you tried to fit in a piano, there wouldn't be any room left for us and our clothes."

"But think what fun we'd have," said Shanon. "Every evening we could all gather around the piano and sing. That's what your Gammy says they used to do for entertainment. They weren't allowed to have radios or record players."

"Right," said Lisa. "There weren't any TVs or CDs or anything. According to Gammy, in the old days the Alma girls spent their spare time drinking tea, playing instruments, and sewing."

"And studying," Shanon put in. "Don't forget that. It was really unusual for girls to go to a school like this in the old days. They had to be really serious."

"But not too serious to write some juicy letters," Lisa added, beaming. She took the newspaper from Amy. "This is my favorite part," she said, reading aloud from Shanon's article: "Mrs. McGreevy, who will celebrate her seventieth birthday this year and whose granddaughter Lisa now attends Alma Stephens, states that her favorite pastime when she was a student here was writing letters. . . ."

"Here comes Palmer," Amy suddenly announced, glancing out of the window. Shanon and Lisa joined Amy, and the three girls watched their suitemate come trudging up the path to Fox Hall. There had been a heavy snowfall the night before, and Palmer was carefully maneuvering her way through a big snowdrift.

"Maybe we should go take her some snowshoes," Lisa suggested, following Palmer's slow progress up the walk. "She hates getting her feet wet."

"She's doing fine with those high boots she wore," observed Shanon.

"She must really like that job of hers," Amy said. "Even though the paths weren't shoveled this morning, Palmer was off to The Tuck Shop bright and early."

"Mrs. Butter says Palmer's a good worker," Shanon told them. "And Palmer really seems to like her job now— although she has been kind of quiet since the day we brought Sam there."

Lisa turned back toward her grandmother's trunk. "At least she's forgiven us for inviting him," she said, pulling out the big petticoat. "She understands that we were trying to do something nice for her."

Shanon sighed. "Too bad our plan backfired."

"Shh!" Lisa hissed as Palmer walked into the suite.

"It's great out there," Palmer announced, her face glowing from the cold.

"Huh?" said Lisa. "We saw you. You almost fell into a snowdrift."

Palmer shrugged. "I like snow."

"How about some hot chocolate?" Amy offered.

111

"In a minute," Palmer said good-naturedly. She threw off her big down coat and began working on her boots.

"Did your socks get wet, Palmer?" Shanon asked. "Let me get you some dry ones."

"Look, Palmer," Lisa said, "Gammy sent a petticoat. I thought you might like it."

"There's a parasol for you, too," exclaimed Amy. "We thought you'd be the perfect person to carry it."

Palmer pulled off one of her light blue socks and looked up at her suitemates. Shanon had some dry socks in her hand, Lisa was holding the petticoat, and Amy the parasol. "You guys don't have to be so nice to me," Palmer said. "I'm not depressed or anything."

"We're glad you're not depressed," Amy said, "but you have been having some bad luck."

"Not anymore," Palmer told them.

The three girls followed her with their eyes as Palmer sauntered into her bedroom.

"You got some good news?" Lisa asked. "Tell us."

"Yes, what happened?" Amy asked curiously.

Palmer reappeared in the doorway. "I had a meeting with Mr. Griffith this morning after I got off work," she announced with a smile. "And I'm off academic warning!"

"That's awesome!" cried Amy.

"Great!" Shanon agreed.

"And quick, too," Lisa chimed in. "Your grades must be really coming up."

"It's slow going," Palmer admitted, "but they're definitely improving."

"Enough for Mr. Griffith to take you off warning," Shanon said encouragingly.

The girls were so busy congratulating Palmer they almost

didn't hear the soft knock at the door. But they all smiled when Kate poked her head in. She was wearing the leopardskin pillbox hat she'd bought at Palmer's tag sale.

"Hey," laughed Amy, "you're just in time for the costume party!"

"I thought I'd at least try this dumb hat out," Kate said, blushing. "After all, I paid a dollar for it."

"It looks kind of good on you," Lisa offered.

"Better than it did on my mother," said Palmer with a giggle. "It was a little too small for her head and it always looked like it was just about to fall off. That's why she gave it to me."

Kate smiled, then blushed, then smiled again. "Oops!" she said, "I almost forgot why I'm here." She thrust some envelopes at Lisa. "The mail came."

"Mail!" yelped Amy. "I thought for sure today's delivery wouldn't come through."

"You know the old saying," Kate said. "Neither rain, nor snow, nor hail, nor . . . well, you know the rest," she added. "See you later!"

"Thanks, Kate," said Shanon. "I'll see you at *The Ledger* office. I'm coming over right after I do the books for The Tuck Shop."

"Who's the mail for?" Amy asked as soon as the door closed behind Kate.

"All three letters are for Palmer," Lisa said, handing over the envelopes.

"For me?" said Palmer, quickly checking the return addresses. One was from Florida and one was from California. "Uh-oh," she said, "Mom and Dad both wrote to me." She picked up the third letter. "And, oh, my gosh! This one's from Sam."

113

"From Sam?" exclaimed Shanon.

"Open it up!" said Lisa.

"I don't know if I want to," said Palmer. "The last letter he sent me was bad enough. What if he's writing to say he hates me because I ruined his jeans?"

"Why don't you open the letters from your parents first," Amy suggested. "They've already cut off your allowance. Nothing could be worse than that."

"Right," said Palmer, ripping open the envelopes. She read the letters from her parents and passed them around.

Dear Palmer,

I am very happy that your grades are improving. I am reinstating your allowance.

> *Love,*
> *Mom*

P.S. I love you for yourself. You are not a disappointment to me! In the whole world there is only one Palmer Durand!

Dear Palmer,

I am proud of the way you've improved in your school-work. And I am sorry that I haven't had time to communicate with you more often. Maybe I should go back to school to learn how to be a better parent. I am also sorry that we cannot turn back the clock and have things the way they were when you were little. But please remember that I love you and am glad you are my daughter.

> *Love,*
> *Dad*

P.S. Enclosed is your allowance—plus a little bonus for all the hard work you've been putting in lately.

"Fantastic!" yelled Lisa.

Palmer's eyes misted over. "Those are the nicest letters my parents ever wrote me! Not only that," she added happily, "I've got my allowance back!"

"Yeah!" said Amy. "You're rich again!"

"Now let's see the letter from Sam," said Lisa.

Palmer opened Sam's letter with trembling hands, but a big smile spread across her face as she began to read.

Dear Palmer,

The reason I came to The Tuck Shop was that I wanted to speak to you. But then I got embarrassed. I just want you to know that if we aren't pen pals anymore, it isn't really because I want it that way. I just thought that if you wanted me to be an Ardie so bad that you had to tell your father that I was one, then maybe you would be happier getting a real Ardie for your pen pal. But if that isn't it, then I would like to keep writing to you. Please answer and tell me how you feel about all this.

Yours truly,
Sam

"He wants to be your pen pal again!" cried Amy.

"That's nice," Palmer said. She took the three letters and carefully folded them back into their envelopes.

"Gee," said Lisa, "if I were you I'd be jumping up and down now."

"Don't get me wrong," said Palmer with a big smile, "I'm really glad about everything. But I've been feeling different lately. I kind of realized something." She paused to find the words for what she wanted to say. "I felt really bad last week when Sam didn't say anything to me at The Tuck Shop," she went on slowly. "And you know how bummed out I was about my parents. But lately I've been feeling good about making it on my own. You know what I mean?"

"I think so," said Shanon.

"Everything's turned out great," said Lisa. "This calls for something to eat."

"I have just the thing!" Amy said, dashing out the door. "It's in the dorm kitchen!"

"So are you going to keep your job at The Tuck Shop?" Shanon asked Palmer.

"You might as well quit," said Lisa. "You don't need the money anymore."

"I don't think I'll be quitting for a while," Palmer told them. "I got paid today!"

"But you've got your allowance back," Lisa argued. "What are you going to do with all that money?"

Palmer shrugged. "Buy two skirts instead of one, I guess. I don't know," she added, flushing, "maybe I'll save it. Anyway, don't forget—I don't just get money at The Tuck Shop. I get free ice cream!"

Amy came in carrying a tray with a basket of fruit and another pitcher of hot chocolate.

"Wow, where did you get that great-looking fruit?" asked Lisa.

"My parents sent it from home," Amy replied. "It was left over from my family's New Year's celebration."

"I never heard how that went," Palmer said. "I was so busy thinking about my own problems I didn't even ask."

Amy shrugged and grabbed a piece of round yellowish fruit from the basket. It looked like a gigantic grapefruit. "I still don't think Mom and Dad would be too happy if I became a rock star," she said, "but at least they understand I'm serious about music now."

116

"All right!" said Lisa. "That's progress!"

"It sure is," said Amy. "I even sang a song to my father."

"And?" asked Shanon.

"He liked it," said Amy. She slowly peeled the thick skin off the yellow fruit. Then, breaking it into sections, she passed some around.

"Yum," said Lisa, licking the juice off her fingers. "What is this?"

"It tastes like grapefruit," observed Shanon.

"I like it," said Palmer, nibbling.

"It's called pomelo," Amy said, serving herself a piece of the fruit. "We eat it on Chinese New Year. It's a symbol of family togetherness."

"Neat," said Lisa, grabbing another piece.

"And delicious," agreed Shanon.

Palmer and Amy smiled at each other and took some more. For a while there were only the sounds of eating and drinking.

"A symbol of family togetherness, huh?" Palmer finally murmured.

Amy smiled and nodded. Then Lisa smiled at Shanon. Still slurping the juicy fruit, the four Foxes all looked at each other. Nobody said anything else, but they all knew they were thinking the same thing. Even though they hadn't grown up in the same house, in some magic way they were a family.

CHAPTER SEVENTEEN

Dear Amy,

It was great seeing you at the Centennial Weekend. Hope we don't have to wait a hundred years to meet again. Keep writing!

Yours truly,
John

Dear Lisa,

I hope we didn't get you in trouble with Palmer by bringing Sam to Alma Stephens. Your painting looks like it could have been done by a lady Vincent Van Gogh. I'm impressed.

Catch you later,
Rob

Dear Shanon,

I just want to tell you how cool it was to see you. You are a brain! What a great idea to interview Lisa's grandmother for your article. Maybe next time you can interview me! I

118

don't know about what yet—but I'm sure we'll think of something worth writing about!

> Your wild and crazy pen pal,
> Mars

Dear Sam,

I got your letter, and I would definitely like to still be pen pals. Thank you for not being mad at me for lying. I think you are a great person no matter where you go to school.

> Yours truly,
> Palmer

P.S. I got my allowance back, but I am still a waitress.

Dear Palmer,

I'm glad you have your allowance back. Even though you spilled ice cream on me, I'm sure you're a great waitress. Most of all I'm glad we're still pen pals.

> Love,
> Sam

P.S. Keep those letters coming!

Something to write home about . . .
                    another new Pen Pals story!

In Book Eleven, *Roommate Trouble*, Lisa rearranges the suite so that all four girls sleep together in the sitting room. And when shy Muffin Talbot complains that Lorraine Murphy, her new roommate, is a monster, Lisa invites her to sleep in the suite, too. Soon Suite 3-D is so crowded Shanon can hardly study, so she studies in Lorraine's room—and starts to like Lorraine. But her suitemates, especially Lisa, think Lorraine is taking advantage of Shanon.

P.S. Have you missed any Pen Pals? Catch up now!

PEN PALS #1: BOYS WANTED!

Suitemates Lisa, Shanon, Amy, and Palmer love the Alma Stephens School for Girls. There's only one problem—no boys! So the girls put an ad in the newspaper of the nearby Ardsley Academy for Boys asking for male pen pals. Soon their mailboxes are flooded with letters and photos from Ardsley boys, but the girls choose four boys from a suite just like their own. Through their letters, the girls learn a lot about their new pen pals—and about themselves.

PEN PALS #2: TOO CUTE FOR WORDS

Palmer, the rich girl from Florida, has never been one for playing by the rules. So when she wants Amy's pen pal, Simmie, instead of her own, she simply takes him. She writes to Simmie secretly and soon he stops writing to Amy. When Shanon, Lisa, and Amy find out why, the suite is in an uproar. How could Palmer be so deceitful? Before long, Palmer is thinking of leaving the suite—and the other girls aren't about to stop her. Where will it all end?

PEN PALS #3: P.S. FORGET IT!

Palmer is out to prove that her pen pal is the best—and her suitemate Lisa's is a jerk. When Lisa receives strange letters and a mysterious prank gift, it looks as if Palmer may be right. But does she have to be so smug about it? Soon it's all-out war in Suite 3-D!

From the sidelines, Shanon and Amy think something fishy is going on. Is the pen pal scheme going too far? Will it stop before Lisa does something she may regret? Or will the girls learn to settle their differences?

PEN PALS #4: NO CREEPS NEED APPLY

Palmer takes up tennis so she can play in the Alma-Ardsley tennis tournament with her pen pal, Simmie Randolph III. Lisa helps coach Palmer, and soon Palmer has come so far that they are both proud of her. But when Palmer finds herself playing *against*—not *with*—her super-competitive pen pal, she realizes that winning the game could mean losing *him*!

Palmer wants to play her best, and her suitemates will

think she's a real creep if she lets down the school. Is any boy worth the loss of her friends?

PEN PALS #5: SAM THE SHAM

Palmer has a new pen pal. His name is Sam O'Leary, and he seems absolutely perfect! Palmer is walking on air. She can't think or talk about anything but Sam—even when she's supposed to be tutoring Gabby, a third-grader from town, as part of the school's community-service requirement. Palmer thinks it's a drag, until she realizes just how much she means to little Gabby. And just in time, too—she needs something to distract her from her own problems when it appears that there *is* no Sam O'Leary at Ardsley. But if that's the truth—who *has* been writing to Palmer?

PEN PALS #6: AMY'S SONG

The Alma Stephens School is buzzing with excitement—the girls are going to London! Amy is most excited of all. She and her pen pal John have written a song together, and one of the Ardsley boys has arranged for her to sing it in a London club. It's the chance of a lifetime! But once in London, the girls are constantly supervised, and Amy can't see how she'll ever get away to the club. She and her suite-mates plot and scheme to get out from under the watchful eye of their chaperone, but it's harder than they thought it would be. It looks as if Amy will never get her big break!

PEN PALS #7: HANDLE WITH CARE

Shanon is tired of standing in Lisa's shadow. She wants to be thought of as her own person. So she decides to run for

Student Council representative—against Lisa! Lisa not only feels abandoned by her best friend, but by her pen pal, too. While the election seems to be bringing Shanon and Mars closer together, it's definitely driving Lisa and Rob apart. Lisa's sure she'll win the election. After all, she's always been a leader—shy Shanon's the follower. Or is she? Will the election spoil the girls' friendship? And will it mean the end of Rob and Lisa?

PEN PALS #8: SEALED WITH A KISS

When the Ardsley and Alma drama departments join forces to produce a rock musical, Lisa and Amy audition just for fun. Lisa lands a place in the chorus, but Amy gets a leading role. Lisa can't help feeling a little jealous, especially when her pen pal Rob also gets a leading role—opposite Amy. To make matters worse, the director wants Rob and Amy to kiss! Amy is so caught up in the play that she doesn't notice Lisa's jealousy—at first. And when she finally does notice, the damage has already been done! Is it too late to save their friendship?

PEN PALS #9: STOLEN PEN PALS

Shanon, Lisa, Amy, and Palmer have been very happy with their pen pals—but now they have competition! Four very preppy—and very pretty—girls from Brier Hall have advertised for Ardsley pen pals. And pen pals they get—including Rob, Mars, and John! Soon the boys are living at the rival school as part of an exchange program—and the Fox Hall suitemates' mailboxes are empty. The girls may have had their differences, but there's one thing they can agree on: Brier Hall must be stopped!

WANTED: BOYS — AND GIRLS —
WHO CAN WRITE !

Join the Pen Pals Exchange and get a pen pal of your own!
Fill out the form below.
Send it with a self-addressed stamped envelope to:

PEN PALS EXCHANGE
c/o The Trumpet Club
PO Box 632
Holmes, PA 19043
U.S.A.

In a couple of weeks you'll receive the name and address
of someone who wants to be your pen pal.

Cut here ---

PEN PALS EXCHANGE

NAME _____   GRADE _____

ADDRESS _____

TOWN _____   STATE _____   ZIP _____

DON'T FORGET TO INCLUDE A STAMPED ENVELOPE
WITH YOUR NAME AND ADDRESS ON IT!